W9-DAW-239

La's Orchestra Saves
the World

BOOKS BY ALEXANDER McCALL SMITH

IN THE ISABEL DALHOUSIE SERIES
The Sunday Philosophy Club
Friends, Lovers, Chocolate
The Right Attitude to Rain
The Careful Use of Compliments
The Comforts of a Muddy Saturday

IN THE NO. 1 LADIES' DETECTIVE AGENCY SERIES
The No. 1 Ladies' Detective Agency
Tears of the Giraffe
Morality for Beautiful Girls
The Kalahari Typing School for Men
The Full Cupboard of Life
In the Company of Cheerful Ladies
Blue Shoes and Happiness
The Good Husband of Zebra Drive
The Miracle at Speedy Motors
Tea Time for the Traditionally Built

IN THE PORTUGUESE IRREGULAR VERBS SERIES
Portuguese Irregular Verbs
The Finer Points of Sausage Dogs
At the Villa of Reduced Circumstances

IN THE 44 SCOTLAND STREET SERIES
44 Scotland Street
Espresso Tales
Love over Scotland
The World According to Bertie

The Girl Who Married a Lion and Other Tales from Africa

ALEXANDER
McCALL SMITH

La's Orchestra Saves the World

Alfred A. Knopf Canada

2009

This book is for J. K. Mason

PUBLISHED BY ALFRED A. KNOPF CANADA

Copyright © 2009 Alexander McCall Smith

www.randomhouse.ca

Library and Archives Canada Cataloguing in Publication

McCall Smith, Alexander, 1948–
La's orchestra saves the world / Alexander McCall Smith.

ISBN 978-0-307-39811-6

I. Title.

PR6063.C326L38 2009   823'.914   C2008-907097-6

Typeset in Minion by Palimpsest Book Production Limited,
Grangemouth, Stirlingshire

First Edition

Printed and bound in the United States of America

10 9 8 7 6 5 4 3 2 1

Part One

One

Two men, who were brothers, went to Suffolk. One drove the car, an old Bristol drophead coupé in British racing green, while the other navigated, using an out-of-date linen-backed map. That the map was an old one did not matter too much: the roads they were following had been there for a long time and were clearly marked on their map – narrow lanes flanked by hedgerows following no logic other than ancient farm boundaries. The road-signs – promising short distances of four miles, two miles, even half a mile – were made of heavy cast-iron, forged to last for generations of travellers. Some conscientious hand had kept them freshly painted, their black lettering sharp and clear against chalk-white backgrounds, pointing to villages with names that meant something a long time ago but which were now detached from the things to which they referred – the names of long-forgotten yeoman families, of mounds, of the crops they grew, of the wild flora of those parts. Garlic, cress, nettles, crosswort – all these featured in the place-names of the farms and villages that dotted the countryside – their comfortable names reminders of a gentle country that once existed in these parts, England. It still survived, of course, tenacious here and there, revealed in a glimpse of a languorous cricket match on a green, of a trout pool under willow branches, of a man in a flat cap digging up potatoes; a country that still existed but was being driven into redoubts such as this. The heart might ache for that England, thought one of the brothers; might ache for what we have lost.

They almost missed the turning to the village, so quickly did it come upon them. There were oak trees at the edge of a field and immediately beyond these, meandering off to the left, was the road leading to the place they wanted. The man with the map shouted out, 'Whoa! Slow down,' and the driver reacted quickly, stamping on the brakes of the Bristol, bringing it to a halt with a faint smell of scorched rubber. They looked at the sign, which was a low one, almost obscured by the topmost leaves of nettles and clumps of cow parsley. It was the place.

It was a narrow road, barely wide enough for two vehicles. Here and there informal passing places had been established by local use – places where wheels had flattened the grass and pushed the hedgerows back a few inches. But you only needed these if there were other road-users, and there were none that Saturday afternoon. People were sleeping, or tending their gardens in the drowsy heat of summer, or perhaps just thinking.

'It's very quiet, isn't it?' remarked the driver when they stopped to check their bearings at the road end.

'That's what I like about it,' said the other man. 'This quietness. Do you remember that?'

'We would never have noticed it. We would have been too young.'

They drove on slowly to the edge of the village. The tower

of a Norman church rose above a stand of alders. In some in-explicable mood of Victorian architectural enthusiasm, a small stone bobble, rather like a large cannonball, had been added at each corner of the tower. These additions were too small to ruin the original proportions, too large to be ignored; Suffolk churches were used to such spoliation, although in the past it had been carried out in a harsh mood of Puritan iconoclasm rather than prettification. There was to be no idolatry here: Marian and other suspect imagery had been rooted out, gouged from the wood of pew-ends and reredoses, chipped from stone baptismal fonts; stained glass survived, as it did here, only because it would be too costly to replace with the clear glass of Puritanism.

Behind the church, the main street, a winding affair, was lined mostly by houses, joined to one another in the cheek-by-jowl democracy of a variegated terrace. Some of these were built of stone, flinted here and there in patterns – triangles, wavy lines; others, of wattle and daub, painted either in cream or in that soft pink which gives to parts of Suffolk its gentle glow. There were a couple of shops and an old pub where a blackboard proclaimed the weekend's fare: hotpot, fish stew, toad-in-the-hole; the stubborn cuisine of England.

'That post office,' said the driver. 'What's happened to it?'

The navigator had folded the map and tucked it away in the leather pocket in the side of the passenger door. He looked at his brother, and he nodded.

'Just beyond the end of the village,' said the driver. 'It's on the right. Just before . . .'

His brother looked at him. 'Just before Ingoldsby's Farm. Remember?'

The other man thought. A name came back to him, dredged up from a part of his memory he did not know he had. 'The Aggs,' he said. 'Mrs Agg.'

She had been waiting for them, they thought, because she opened the door immediately after they rang the bell. She smiled, and gestured for them to come in, with the warmth, the eagerness of one who gets few callers.

'I just remember this house,' the driver said, looking about him. 'Not very well, but just. Because when we were boys,' and he looked at his brother, 'when we were boys we lived here. Until I was twelve. But you forget.'

His brother nodded in agreement. 'Yes. You know how things look different when you're young. They look much bigger.'

She laughed. 'Because at that age one is looking at things from down there. Looking up. I was taken to see the Houses of Parliament when I was a little girl. I remember thinking that the tower of Big Ben was quite the biggest thing I had ever seen in my life – and it might have been, I suppose. But when I went back much later on, it seemed so much smaller. Rather disappointing, in fact.'

She ushered them through the hall into a sanctum beyond, a drawing-room into which French windows let copious amounts of light. Beyond these windows, an expanse of grass stretched out to a high yew hedge, a dark-green backdrop for the herbaceous beds lining the lawn. There was a hedge of lavender, too, grown woody through age.

'That was hers,' said the woman, pointing to the lavender hedge. 'It needs cutting back, but I love it so much I can't bring myself to do it.'

'La planted that?'

'I believe so,' said the woman.

'We played there,' said one of the brothers, looking out into the garden. 'It's odd to think that. But we played there. For hours and hours. Day after day.'

She left them and went to prepare tea. The brothers stood in front of the window.

'What I said about things looking bigger,' one said. 'One might say the same about a person's life, don't you think? A life may look bigger when you're a child, and then later on . . .'

'Narrower? Less impressive?'

'I think so.'

But the other thought that the opposite might be true, at least on occasion. 'A friend told me about a teacher at school,' he said. 'He was a very shy man. Timid. Ineffectual. And children mocked him – you know how quick they are to scent blood in the water. Then, later on, when he met him as an adult, he found out that this same teacher had been a well-known mountaineer and a difficult route had been named after him.'

'And La's life?'

'I suspect that it was a very big one. A very big life led here . . .'

'In this out of the way place.'

'Yes, in this sleepy little village.' He paused. 'I suspect that our La was a real heroine.'

Their hostess had come back into the room, carrying a tray. She put it down on a table and gestured to the circle of chintzy sofa and chairs. She had heard the last remark, and agreed. 'Yes. La was a heroine. Definitely a heroine.'

She poured the tea. 'I assume that you know all about La. After all . . .' She hesitated. 'But then she became ill, didn't she,

not so long after you all left this place. You can't have been all
that old when La died.'

One of the men stared out of the window. The other replied,
'I was seventeen and my brother was nineteen. She was a big
part of our lives. We remember her with . . .'

The older man, still looking out of the window, supplied,
'Love. We remember her with love. And pride, too, I suppose.
But you know how people fade. We wanted to hear what people
here thought. That's why we've come.'

'Of course.'

She looked at them over the rim of her tea-cup. 'By the time
I came to this part of the world you had all gone,' she said. 'I
lived over on the other side of the village. You might have seen
the house as you came in. A bit of a Victorian mistake, now
fortunately mostly covered with ivy. It hides such a multitude
of sins, ivy. So forgiving.'

'I don't remember . . .'

'Look for it on your way out. The person who bought this
house from La – it was a Mrs Dart – came to see me in that
house when I first moved to Suffolk. She welcomed me to the
village. Of course La's orchestra was already a thing of the past
then, but people still talked about it. It was something the village
had done, and they were proud of it.'

'I bought this house from Mrs Dart's estate. They hadn't put
it on the market, and I went to the solicitor who handled her
affairs. He was in Newmarket, so I went there to speak to him
about it. I remember it very well, going into town that morning
when they were exercising the race-horses, a long line of them,
and their breath . . . was like little white clouds. It's a very clear
memory, that has stayed with me.

8

'I still think of this as La's house, you know. And that's what some people in the village still call it – even people who never met La. It's still La's house to them.'

'And her garden,' said the driver.

'Yes. That was so important. And he was responsible for that, you know. During the War, La dug up the lawn and planted whatever it was that she grew. Potatoes, I suppose. Beans. All of that formal garden was taken up, except for a small bit round the side of the house. She kept that as an ornamental garden. Feliks helped.'

'And afterwards, when all the fuss was over and people didn't have to grow so many vegetables, she put that lawn back in, and replaced all the shrubs that she had taken up. She put them all back, in their original spot, working from memory and from photographs.'

They talked. Then, when they had finished their tea, she suggested that they walk the short distance to the church hall.

'It's a tin hall,' she said, as they approached it. 'Made entirely of corrugated tin. You occasionally get that in this county – little tin halls that have withstood the weather, and the years. It was a way of making something reasonably durable on the cheap.'

They stood still for a few minutes and admired the modest building from the end of its path. The walls of tin had been painted in a colour somewhere between ochre and cream, and the roof was rust-red. At one end of the building – the one facing them – there was a small veranda, dominated by a green door. The door, the thin casements of the windows, and the supports under the eaves, were the only wood on the outer surface of the building.

'I have a key,' she said, reaching into a pocket. 'It's a privilege of being on the parish council. We can look inside – not that there's much to see.'

They walked down the path. The lock, an old-fashioned one, was stiff, and had to be coaxed into opening, but at last the door was pushed open and they found themselves standing in a vestibule. There was a notice-board, a square of faded baize, criss-crossed with tape; but no notices; a boot-scraper with bristle and a metal bar. That was all.

She pushed open the inner door, which was unlocked. The air inside was cool, but with a slight musty smell. Light filtered in through small windows that needed cleaning, bars of weak sunlight slanting across the benches stacked along the side of the wall.

'Nowadays,' she said, 'it's used for the school play and the occasional dance. We still have a village dance, you know, in spite of everything. And everybody goes.'

'And the orchestra?'

She gestured about her. 'Under this very roof. Right here. This is where the orchestra played – so I'm told.' She pointed at the windows. 'They were covered, of course. Black-out curtains.'

The driver detached himself and walked to the far end of the hall. The floor underfoot was red-polished concrete of a sort that for some reason he associated with hospitals in foreign countries. He had become sick once as a student, travelling in India, and the hospital ward, with its red concrete floor, had been a little like this.

She spoke to him from the other end of the hall. 'I met somebody who had played here,' she said. 'The orchestra sat over there, where you are now, and when they gave a concert the audience sat at this end. It would have been the whole village, then. Everybody would have come to listen. Everybody.'

He turned round. He looked up at the ceiling, which was made of large expanses of white board nailed onto the roof-beams. The board was discoloured here and there from leaks, brown rings spreading out in concentric circles. He did not think that anything had been painted recently, perhaps not since La's time.

'If you've seen enough,' she said. 'Perhaps we should go back.'

She locked the door behind them, and they walked back in silence, until they had almost reached the house.

'Could you tell me more?' the driver asked. 'About the orchestra?'

He looked up at the sky, which was wide and empty. High above them a line of stratus moved quickly in the air-stream. She followed his gaze. She loved the skies of East Anglia; she loved this flat landscape, which she thought of, in a curious way, as a holy place.

'A bit. Not very much. If you don't mind my being a bit vague.'

'Not at all.' He paused. 'If you have the time.'

She smiled at him. 'In this village, there's not a great deal to do. But remembering is something we're rather good at in these places. Have you noticed that? Go to any small village anywhere in the world, and see what they remember. Everything. It's all there – passed on like a precious piece of information, some secret imparted from one who knew to one who yearns to know. Taken good care of.'

They walked towards the house. The driver touched the Bristol as he passed it, let his fingers brush against the cool of the metal, in a gesture of appreciation that came close, he thought, to talismanic. He had rebuilt the Bristol, part by part, and now he loved it with that very intensity a man might feel for a machine he created himself out of metal, and the things that bind metal.

Two

La's childhood was spent in the shadow of Death. He was an uninvited guest at their table, sitting patiently, watching La's mother, his target, bemused, perhaps, that such courage and determination could keep an illness at bay for so long. But he was in no hurry, and would make his move when every one of the expensive treatments had been tried, and failed. The last of these involved a trip to Switzerland, to a sanatorium near Gstaad, where optimistic doctors prescribed Alpine air and light, but Death accompanied her there too; he was no respecter of altitude and had business with some of the other patients lying on their extended deck chairs. When, shortly after her return to England, the end came, La was just fifteen and at boarding school. The news was broken by a housemistress who found such blows almost impossible to convey, choking with emotion as she spoke, just as La, who had long since realised that this moment was inevitable, and who remained calm, sought to comfort her.

La's father did his best to fill the gap, but it was difficult for him. He was not a demonstrative man, and he simply could not express the love and concern he felt for the child who was the living reminder of his wife in all her gestures and looks. A female child, he felt, needed a woman to look after her, to say and do the things a woman could do. For this reason, he hired a house-keeper who doubled up as mother and, as La realised with shock, as wife. She heard conversation from behind the closed door of her father's bedroom, lowered voices, but in an unmistakeable emotional register. He could not marry her – no, it was impossible. Nobody knew, he said; and even if they did it was none of their business. And why was it impossible? Silence. Was he ashamed of her, of her very ordinary origins? More silence. That's it, isn't it? Ashamed.

The house they lived in was in Surrey, on the brow of a hill. London, or its very fringes, might be seen through the darkness from that vantage point – a low line of lights – and in the day, if conditions were right, it was there as a distant smudge against the horizon. La liked the fact that they lived on a hill, and would introduce herself as one who came from the top of a hill in Surrey.

'I am going to university in a very flat place,' she said to her father. 'You're sending me down from my hill to a very flat place.'

'Cambridge is indeed flat,' he said. 'And . . .' She waited for him to say more, but he often failed to complete these utter-ances. She asked him once what he was thinking of when his sentences petered out, and he had replied, 'Oh, various things, things that . . .'

Cambridge had been La's choice, even if one that had been heavily backed by her English teacher at school, a graduate of Girton. She knew the admissions tutor, she said; they had gone walking in France together as students and she would make sure that any application would be sympathetically viewed. La wondered what that had to do with her; she did not want to be accepted because of some remote bond of friendship, the outcome of a walking tour.

'I'm not saying that,' said the teacher. 'But you'll learn as you go through life that friendship, contacts, call it what you will, lies behind so many of the decisions that people make. It's just the way the world is.'

Girton accepted her, and she began the study of English literature in the autumn of 1929. It seemed that everybody in Cambridge was talking about Mr Leavis, who was on the verge of publishing a great work of criticism, it was said. She met Leavis, and his new wife, Queenie Roth, who talked to her at a party about Jane Austen. It was just one of the heady experiences that Cambridge had in store for La, and it made the hill-top in Surrey seem irredeemably dull.

Her tutor, Dr Price, was ambitious for her. 'You could do a further degree. There's so much to choose from.'

That was not how La saw it. In her view there was so little choice – if one was a woman. 'It's men who have all the oppor-tunities,' she said. 'Look at what they can do. At the most, we have their leavings, the crumbs from their table. It's 1931 and that's all we have. Still.'

'That's because women haven't leaned their lesson,' said the tutor.

'Which is?'

'To live their lives as if men did not exist.'

That was easily said by a tutor in a women's college. But La did not point this out.

'It breaks my heart,' the tutor went on, 'to see all these

intelligent girls come to us and then leave, more or less promised to some man. And they go off and marry him and that's the end. What a waste. What a criminal waste.'

Seeing La's reaction, the tutor offered a list of names. 'Andrews last year; Paterson too, such a brilliant person. Married. Buried away in some dim town somewhere, playing bridge and practising domestic economy. Is that what Cambridge is for?'

La agreed with Dr Price, on that, at least, if not on other matters. She had not come to Cambridge to find a husband; she found it astonishing that there were girls who did just that – she had met some of them, and they admitted it. Our best chance, one said. You'd have to be a fool not to take it. La said nothing; she had come, she believed, to be taught how to think. At school she had been subjected to rote-learning intended to enable her to recite the opinions of others; now she wanted to form her own views, but was finding it difficult. What would these views be, she wondered, once she had formed them?

'Don't you think it exciting, La, to be alive at a time of crisis?'

The speaker was Janey Turner, a young woman who had befriended her at a poetry reading and invited her afterwards to a tea-room. The young men at the reading were hopeless, whispered Janey. 'They're interested only in themselves. Have you noticed that, La? They're all trying to look poetic. All terribly narcissistic and intense. Except for that one who read out the bit about the man in the factory. He understood.'

La wondered about the crisis. Everybody said there was a cultural crisis – that the old certainties had been so destabilised that they were no longer capable of providing any answers. But if that was so, then how were we to know what to believe in? Janey knew the answer, with a confident, complete certainty. The common man, she said. He's the future. We must believe in what he believes in.

'Which is what?'

'The ending of oppression. Freedom from hunger. Freedom from the deception of the Church and the tricks of the ruling class. Flags. National glory. Militarism.'

La pondered this. She agreed that freedom from hunger was an admirable goal – who could take a contrary view on that? And oppression was bad, too; of course it was. But the Church? She thought of the college chaplain, a mild man with a strong interest in Jane Austen and in Tennyson, who was distantly related to Beatrix Potter and who would never have engaged in deception, surely. Or was Janey talking about a different sort of religion altogether? A religion of saints, and icons of saints; of relics and miracles? England, she thought, was not like that.

'Is there a crisis in literature?' La asked Dr Price.

The tutor looked at her as if she had asked an egregiously naïve question. 'Of course. We all know there's a crisis. Everybody.'

Except me, thought La. I'm prepared to accept that there's a crisis – if only somebody would explain how the crisis had come about and just how it manifested itself.

'Why?' she persisted. 'Why is there a crisis?'

Dr Price waved a hand in the air. 'Because of lies and rottenness. Simplicity and sincerity have been replaced by obfuscation and pretence. Men, of course. They love to create mystery where none exists. It's the way they think.'

'So simplicity is a literary virtue?'

Dr Price looked at her severely. 'Yes, of course it is. And it is a virtue that is more assiduously practised by members of our own sex, if I may so.' The severity of her expression slackened, and a smile began to play about her lips. 'Do you know the story about Rupert Brooke's mother? No? Well, let me tell you. She was shown a memoir of her son composed by some man – one Edward Marsh, I believe. He had written: "Rupert Brooke left Rugby in a blaze of glory." And she, the poet's mother, had crossed out *blaze of glory* and substituted *July*.'

Dr Price looked at La. 'You see?' she said.

La found that this conversation, as was the case with many of her discussions with Dr Price, left her dissatisfied. If it was a teacher's role to bring enlightenment, then Dr Price failed in her calling. She behaved as if she were the custodian of a body of knowledge to which her students might aspire, as might one who stumbles upon Eleusinian mysteries yearn to know what is going on. But she did not impart that knowledge willingly.

La was happy enough at Girton, even if she found that the enlightenment she had hoped for was slow to arrive. When she returned after her first long summer vacation, a time spent travelling in Italy with a cousin, she decided that there would be no sudden moment of insight; at the most she would start to see things slightly differently, would understand the complexity that lay below the surface. She did not worry about that. At present she was free to read and to spend long hours in discussion with her fellow undergraduates, talking about what they had read. She joined a music society, and played the flute in a quartet. She had learned the instrument at school, where it had been something of a chore for her. Now she took it up without the pressure of practice and examinations, and found that she enjoyed it. They struggled through Haydn and Mozart, and gave a concert for the junior common room at the end of the term. A young man, Richard Stone, came to that, sitting in a group of young men, wearing a blue cravat that caught La's eye. He was tall, with the confident bearing of an athlete. She looked up from her music at the end of the first piece and noticed him. He caught her eye and smiled. Then at the end of the concert, when they went into a room where tea had been prepared, he came up to her and introduced himself. He was not embarrassed, as some of the men were, but spoke to her as if they already knew one another.

After a few minutes he invited her to come with him and a group of his friends to a picnic at Grantchester. She hesitated for a moment, but only for a moment. She had that afternoon had a particularly unsatisfactory session with Dr Price, who had criticised her essay and hinted that it was the sort of work that would attract, at best, a third. Dr Price did not like men; this was a man asking her to go on a picnic, and so she accepted.

She learned more about Richard from a friend whose brother knew him. He did not have a reputation as a scholar, she was told, but was good-looking and effortlessly popular; he could row, although he would never make the college eight. Too lazy, somebody had said.

'Are you keen on him?' asked the friend who had imparted the information about Richard. 'He's good-looking, isn't he?'

La felt flustered. Richard could be a friend, but she expected nothing more than that. 'He's nice enough. But that's about it.'

'Pity. Because he likes you. It's obvious.'

'Is it?'

The friend laughed. 'Have you seen the way he looks at you?'

La had seen, but had put it down to something else, perhaps to what Dr Price would have described as male arrogance. At the picnic in Grantchester, he had stared at her with a quiet solemnity, as if he had made up his mind about something. But now that her friend had spelled it out, she could hardly not think about it. It had not occurred to her that anybody could admire her in that way. She did not consider herself attractive; I am too tall, she thought. At school a spiteful girl had said to her: 'Boys won't look at you, La. Never. They don't look at tall girls. Know that?'

She had grown up with the assumption that this was true and had decided that if a boy came along, one she liked, she would have to do the pursuing. But that was not yet. That would be at some unspecified time in the future, when she was twenty-eight, thirty perhaps. I will not let it become anything more than what it is, she told herself. I have not come here to find a husband.

They went to their picnic, and to another one after that.

'I like sitting in fields,' said Richard, and laughed.

He took her to tea, and started cycling out to see her every afternoon. Soon she came to expect him, just after four o' clock, even in the rain, to which he seemed indifferent. 'Just water,' he said. 'And you look nice when you're bedraggled.'

They talked to each other easily, as if they were old friends. In the cinema he took her hand and then kissed her. He tasted of tobacco, and she imagined, absurdly, that she might reveal this to Dr Price in one of their uncomfortable meetings. 'Do you know, Dr Price, that men taste of *tobacco*? Did you know that?'

Six weeks after their first meeting, he had told her that he hoped she would marry him; he would be honoured, he said. 'I've never proposed to anybody before. I really haven't.'

She almost laughed. There was a seriousness about the way

he spoke which made her think he was reciting lines that somebody had taught him; perhaps she might find the very play from
which they were lifted. 'It's very sudden.' That was all she could
think of to say, trite as it was.

'Which means yes? Please tell me that this means yes. If you
had wanted to say no, then you would have said it. Anything
else must mean yes – it must.'

She wanted to be firm, but it was difficult. There was something winning about his manner that made him hard to resist;
he was like an eager schoolboy. 'I don't know. You can't expect
somebody to make up her mind just like that. It's been five
weeks.'

'Six. Almost seven. And I knew immediately. I really did, you
know. I was quite certain that you were the one. You have to
marry me.'

Now she laughed, and he had taken that as her answer. In her
first private moment thereafter, she looked into a mirror, staring
at herself, wide-eyed. You are a person to whom another person
has proposed. It seemed absurd; risible. She had laughed earlier
on, immediately after he had declared himself, but her laughter
had been taken as some sort of assent. She would have to clear
it up; she would have to sit Richard down and talk to him seriously. She would brush aside his persuasive banter and get to the
essential point: she was not ready to get married. They could get
to know one another better and there was always the possibility
that at some point their friendship might become something
more, but not now.

She tried that, but he seemed not to take her seriously. 'Fine,'
he said. 'Fine. We can think about things. Plenty of time for that.
But you and I know how we feel, don't we?'

'Well, frankly, Richard, I'm not sure that you know how I feel. If only you would listen to me . . .'

But as the months went past, and they still saw one another every day, meeting in that small tea-shop off King's Parade, where the waitresses, who seemed fond of him, addressed him as 'Dickie', she found that her feelings were changing. She looked forward to their meetings now; counted the hours and minutes before they would be together again. Was this what it meant to *fall* for somebody? She believed it was. And if she had to marry *someone* – and she mostly assumed that she did – then would she ever find anybody quite as charming as Richard? He would be kind to her. They would have fun together. Could one ever really expect anything more than that out of marriage?

Her father approved of Richard; approved of what he described as his prospects. Richard was going into the family firm of wine merchants – not just any wine merchants, but substantial ones, with connections to the port trade as well. They had their own warehouse in Bordeaux and a share in another one on the Douro. And Richard charmed him, as he could charm anybody, simply by smiling. He did not have to say anything; he merely allowed his smile to work for him. It disarmed.

'I'm so happy for you, my dear,' her father said. 'After all that sadness, the business with your mother, and all that . . .'

'I'm glad that you like him. He's a nice boy, isn't he?'

His father waved a hand in the air. 'Of course. But you never would . . .'

She waited. What would she never do? Choose the wrong sort of man?

Richard was not that; she was sure of it. He was gentle, and amusing, and so she said yes, she would marry him. Later.

He looked at her earnestly. 'After we leave Cambridge?'

'Of course.'

'June, then.'

She had not meant it to be that soon, but he was impossible to argue with. She acquiesced. What difference did it make, now that her future was to be with him.

Her friend Janey, the one who had taken her to the poetry reading, quizzed her. 'Are you completely sure?' she asked.

'Yes. I suppose I am.'

Janey frowned. 'Not suppose. You shouldn't say "suppose". People who are madly in love with another person never say "I suppose I love him." They just don't.'

La thought out loud. 'I do love him. We laugh at the same things. He's kind. What more could one ask for?'

'Romance,' said Janey. 'Passion. An aching for the other person. An emptiness in his absence. That sort of thing.'

'Maybe,' said La. 'Anyway, we're getting married.'

The marriage took place in the chapel of St John's, his college. La's small family, her father, his brother and sister, a few distant cousins, filled a couple of pews; Richard's list was much longer, and included numerous school friends. They gave him a party the night before and threw him in the river, ruining his blazer.

La felt a strange, unaccustomed tenderness for him at the altar, noticing the nervous trembling of his hands as he slipped the ring onto her finger. 'It's all right,' she whispered.

'I'm so happy,' he whispered back.

After the honeymoon, they went to London, staying first in a flat in Fitzrovia that Richard's father had rented for them. Then, a few months later, Richard paid a deposit for the purchase of a house in Maida Vale that was too large for them, but which had a long strip of garden that La started to cultivate. He was now working in the family firm, a job that allowed him to leave the office at four in the afternoon if he wished. La wanted to work, but received little encouragement from Richard.

'Why?' he asked. 'Why work when you don't have to? We've got enough – more than enough. Why shut yourself up in an office with a lot of silly girls?'

She looked at him. 'Not all of them would be silly.'

'Yes, of course.' He smiled. 'Sorry.'

'I don't want to spend my life sitting about. I want to earn my keep.'

'But that's what I'm doing. I'm earning your keep.'

She shook her head. 'You know that's not the same. I want to do something with my life.'

He seemed genuinely puzzled. 'But you are doing something. You're my wife. That's something, isn't it?'

She did not think that was enough, but did not say anything.

'And there'll be children,' he added, reaching out to touch her arm. 'Soon enough.'

They had not discussed this; nothing had been said. It would be something that just happened, and she was not sure how she felt about it. One part of her wanted to be a mother; another understood that that would really be the end of her hopes to do something more with her life. But as the months wore on and nothing happened, she began to wonder whether that would happen. Still nothing was said.

They went to the theatre, to concerts, to the opera; Richard indulged her in all of these, although his tastes were not musical. 'That part's missing in my brain,' he said. 'I hear the notes, but they don't mean very much to me.'

'Are you happy?' her father asked her on an occasion when they met for lunch in town. 'You look happy, I must say.'

'Of course I am,' said La.

'And Richard too?'

'Very. He doesn't talk about happiness, of course. Men tend not to. Men don't talk about their feelings.'

Her father nodded. 'So true. And yet men have feelings, I think, in much the same way as . . .' He looked out of the restaurant, at the passers-by in the street outside. Some of them looked worn-out, ground-down by what he called *general conditions*. 'General conditions are so . . .' he said.

La knew what he meant. She felt guilty that she should be comfortable when others were suffering. 'What can one do?' she asked her father.

'Not much. If you gave your money away it would be gone in a puff of smoke and not make much difference to anybody. So just concentrate on small, immediate things. They make a difference to the world.'

'But look what's happening in Spain and Germany.'

He did not think that there was too much cause to worry. 'Spain's Spain, and always has been. They're cruel. They've always been cruel – and not just to those unfortunate bulls. Germany is full of militaristic bravado,' he added. 'But they're weak. Our Empire is so much bigger, so much more solid. They've got nothing really. No wonder they go on about *Lebensraum* . . .'

La had never taken a very close interest in politics, but she read the newspapers and now it was impossible to be indifferent to what was happening. She took to attending lectures on economics and unemployment, and she felt the sense of outrage that gripped the audience. It was intolerable that people should be deprived of the fundamental dignity of being able to work for a living. Everybody was suffering, she read, but she did not think this was true. She and Richard were still well-off; it was something to do with not having too much invested in the stock exchange, Richard said, and in the continued demand for good wine.

She volunteered to teach a course in literature for the Workers' Educational Association. Richard did not like her going off to the East End alone, but she did nonetheless, and became involved in a parish soup kitchen and in a team that assisted a nurse to inspect the heads of children for lice and to shave their hair. The children were dirty and her hands would smell after the smaller ones had taken them and clasped them. They wanted affection, these children, and she embraced them. 'Careful,' said the nurse. 'Check your own hair, Mrs Stone.'

'We are at the centre of the greatest empire the world has ever known, Sister Edwards. And yet there's all this want. Look at it.'

'It's always been like that, Mrs Stone. Nothing's changed, has it?'

Richard said: 'I'm not happy about all this, La. You have everything you need. I know that things are bad for some, but there's not much we can do, is there? You don't have to spend so much time trying to change things, you know.'

They disagreed on this, but La's view prevailed. Her feelings for Richard had changed over the first year of their marriage; she was used to him now, and the fondness she felt for him had deepened. She began to worry about him, to feel anxious if he was late home. She took his hand at odd moments and held it to her breast. 'I do love you, you know,' she said. 'So much. You know that, don't you?'

He smiled. 'Strange woman.'

'Strange that I should love you?'

He winked. 'Maybe.'

She went to a doctor, discreetly, without telling him that she had made the appointment. The doctor said, 'It's difficult to tell. People can wait for years, you know, and then suddenly a child comes along. We can do some investigation, of course. But it may not reveal anything.'

But it did. The doctor, who understood these things, who knew that the wife might not want the husband to know, did not write her a letter, but waited for her to telephone back for an appointment.

'It's not good news, I'm afraid, Mrs Stone.'

She left his surgery and walked back along the street, past the underground station where she should have caught her train. She walked on, along unfamiliar pavements in the hinterland of Harley Street. One future had closed to her with the doctor's few words.

She told Richard. He seemed surprised that she had consulted the doctor without telling him.

'You should have spoken to me about it, La,' he said. 'I'm your husband, for God's sake.'

'We never spoke,' she said. 'I always felt it was a subject you didn't want to address. I'm sorry if I was wrong about that.'

He spoke angrily. 'You were.'

'I'm very sorry. And it's my fault that we can't have children.'

He softened. 'It's not your fault. It's not.'

'Well, put it this way – I'm the reason.'

'It doesn't matter. Come here.' He put his arms around her. 'I have you and you have me. That's enough, isn't it?'

She wept, and he comforted her. This whole experience, painful though it was, brought them closer together and she thought, *I am truly in love with him. Truly. I know it now.*

Now it seemed that Richard provoked a far more profound need within her. She wanted to be with him; she wanted all his attention; she wanted him to feel about her what she found herself feeling about him. He had suddenly become so important to her that even his possessions seemed to have gathered an aura about them; his handkerchiefs – *his* – his leather key wallet, his jacket; simple, everyday things, but now endowed with a mystical weight beyond their ordinary function. She asked herself how other people – people who came into contact with him at the office, for instance – could not feel the same way about him. Could they not *sense* it? Surely everyone, all of humanity, must succumb to his charms as she had; must understand how completely special he was.

She marvelled at her discovery. It was the most universal of human emotions – love – but now, for the first time, she knew what it meant. It imbued everything with value and a sort of rare excitement; made each day into something precious, a gift.

She could not tell him how she felt; she had no words for it. She could say *I love you so much*, but what would that convey? People said that all the time – she herself had said it – but they could not possibly be feeling what she felt, or feeling it with the same intensity. And so she used simple words, the formality of which somehow seemed more fitting. 'Thank you for marrying me,' she said.

And he replied: 'I am the one who should thank you. I am the fortunate one.'

She smiled. 'Can you imagine what it must be like to be

unhappy? To live with somebody whom you can't stand any more? Imagine that?'

He closed his eyes for a moment as he thought of this; then opened them and smiled his disarming smile. 'Difficult,' he said quietly.

Three

Richard explained to her what he did at the office. 'It's not very complicated,' he said. 'It's exactly what my father did and my grandfather too, when they were my age. We have agents over in Bordeaux who buy the wine for us. We arrange to ship it and put it in our cellars here in London. Then we sell it to smaller merchants. To hotels. To people who buy directly from us for their own cellars. That's all. My job is to see that it's looked after once it's landed here. I also check the inventories and arrange the tastings.'

'It must be interesting,' she said. 'You must have to keep a lot of figures in your head.'

He looked at her. He raised an eyebrow. 'Hardly. But yes, it has its moments, like any job, I suppose.'

He showed her an album of photographs that his father had built up. There was a photograph of their office in Bordeaux itself – a building with the family name painted on the front and a staff of six or seven men, formally dressed, standing outside. They looked hot in their dark suits and waistcoats in the bright sunlight, but were smiling dutifully. At the edge of the picture, under the shade of a tree, two small boys were playing what looked like a game of marbles, unconcerned by the world of adults. Her eye took in the small details: the boys at their game, the pollarded tree beside the office building, the short shadows which told her that the photograph had been taken around noon.

Then there were the photographs of the *châteaux*. The name of each, or of their place, was written in ink under the photograph, and she took pleasure in uttering them: d'Yquem, Bel-Air, Phélan-Ségur, de Sours. Richard knew most of them. He had spent the last few summers there, working with the agents. He knew a lot of the people in the photographs, and he named them or pointed things out. 'That man has a wooden leg. *Blessé de guerre*, you know. That fellow, they say, has the best palate in the Medoc. That man there is the brother of a bishop.'

'Could we go there?' she asked.

He seemed hesitant; almost as if the world they were looking at was a private one, something just for him. But then he said, 'Of course we can. One of these days.'

They had been married two years, when his father, Gerald, one afternoon came to the house. When she answered the door and saw him standing there, his expression grave, she knew immediately that Richard was dead – there could be no other explanation for such a call. There had been an accident, and Richard was dead.

She felt her legs give way underneath her, and she cried out. Gerald, who had been carrying his umbrella, dropped it and reached out, managing to catch her under the arms as she sagged forward. There was a rending of material as her blouse tore.

'My dear,' he said. 'My dear.'

'He's dead.'

'No, my dear. No. No.'

He helped her to a chair in the hall. She had taken in his denial and looked up at him as one who has been reprieved.

'Why have you come here?'

He knelt beside her so that his face was at her level. He was always impeccably groomed, his thick, dark hair swept neatly to each side of a railroad-straight parting. There was the smell of the pomade that he always used, something with bay rum in it.

'I'm afraid that something has indeed happened,' he said. 'But there has not been an accident. Richard is not dead.'

She stared at him mutely. He looked down at the floor, and rose back to his feet; a joint clicked somewhere. His hand was resting upon her shoulder.

'What has happened, my dear, is that my son . . .' He paused. There was pain in his voice. 'My son, I'm sorry to say, has let us all down. He has left the country and gone to France. On the boat train. This morning. I am very, very sorry to have to tell you this.'

She tried to make sense of what he was saying. Richard had said something about the Medoc. The Medoc? Had he gone there?

'He's gone to the office over there? Is that it?'

Gerald sighed. 'I'm afraid that it's not that innocent. I wish to God it were. He has gone to France, but I'm sorry to say that he has gone because there is a woman there. He informed me this morning, presented me with a *fait accompli*. He did not have the courage to tell you and left me to do it. My son did that. He did that.'

*   *   *

Richard's mother appeared half an hour later. She had been weeping and her eyes were red. She insisted that La should go home with them; they could not countenance her staying by herself. La said nothing, but packed a bag mutely, automatically. It was as if somebody else was going through the physical motions; she felt completely numb, as if she had been disembodied.

She found it difficult to say very much, and did not want to talk. But the following day, tired to the point of exhaustion through lack of sleep, she started to ask them questions. Where had he gone? They believed that it was Margaux. And the woman? She was somebody he had met when he had worked in the office in Bordeaux. She was the daughter of a business acquaintance, the owner of a vineyard there, who had interests in la Rochelle as well. Shipping, they thought. We shall never deal with them again; never.

'You had no idea that there was somebody else?' This was from his mother.

'Of course not? How could I?'

'She had been coming to London on and off. He confessed that to me,' said Gerald.

That silenced her. There had been nights when he had had late meetings – or so he said – and had stayed in his club. And she recalled that weekend when he had gone to watch a rugby game in Cardiff; he would have had the opportunity.

'He took long lunch breaks,' Gerald began. 'Perhaps . . .' But he was silenced by a look from his wife, who glanced anxiously at La.

'I'm going to France,' announced Gerald. 'I'm going to bring him back. I'll drag him back if necessary.'

La shook her head. 'I don't think that you can,' she said. 'And if he doesn't want to be with me, then I wouldn't want him brought back.'

Gerald looked awkward. 'Do you want to divorce him?'

'I suppose I'll have to,' La replied.

'We'll support you in every way,' said Gerald. 'His share in the business will be made over to you. I've already informed our solicitors. They know what the position is. I still control everything.'

'All in good time,' said Richard's mother. 'He might change his mind. We can hope.'

'No,' said Gerald. 'We can't.'

La watched them. Of the two, she thought, I feel sorrier for her. A man can divorce his son if pushed to that extreme; a mother could never do that.

She went back to the house in Maida Vale. A friend from school days, Valerie, a woman who had married a banker and who lived in a flat in Chelsea, came and stayed for a few days. It was a help to have somebody with her, especially an old friend. Valerie talked when she wanted to talk, and was silent when she wanted to be silent. She made no attempts at reassurance, but was direct and pragmatic. 'Bad choice,' she said. 'Bad luck. It could happen to anybody. It's not your fault at all. It's men. That's what they do. All the time. He's not going to come back – not after doing this. So you'll have to forget him, I'm afraid.'

'I suppose you're right.'

'Of course I'm right.'

Valerie lit a cigarette. 'And now?'

'I want to get out of this place. I don't want to live here.'

Valerie looked thoughtful. 'You could stay with us if you like,' she said. 'We've got a spare room. I don't see why you couldn't stay with us . . . for a while. Eventually we'd get on one another's nerves, I suppose, but you could stay with us.'

La laughed. It was the first time that she had laughed since it happened, ten days ago, and it felt strange; as if her face was cracking. 'It would be like being back at school,' she said. 'But different. There'd be a man drifting around.'

'I mean the invitation. I really do.'

'I know.' She stretched out and put a hand on her friend's arm. 'I'm very grateful. But no, I don't think it would be a good idea. They . . . Richard's parents, have offered me something, and I think I'm going to accept. They have a house they never use. It's in the family. They said that I could have it if I wished.'

Valerie blew smoke into the air. 'Here in London?'

'No. It's in the country. In Suffolk. In a village there.'

Valerie frowned. 'You can't go and live in the country. You can't go and bury yourself out there. Suffolk. It's miles away. For God's sake, La!'

'Perhaps I want to be miles away,' said La. 'Perhaps that's exactly what I want . . . now.'

'What will you do?'

'I'll find something,' she said. 'Go for walks. Listen to music. Talk to people.'

'But everybody will be ancient.'

La smiled. 'There are people our age in the country. Bags of them.'

Valerie was not impressed with the argument. 'Yes, but will you understand anything of what they say? Will you?'

'You forget that I come from a hill top in Surrey,' said La. 'From the top of a hill.'

Valerie laughed. La had always entertained her, with her dry sense of humour. She loved her. She would go and stay with her wherever she was, she decided; on the top of a hill, in a valley somewhere; in a sleepy village with incomprehensible locals. Anywhere.

Four

Standing before her new front door, with its peeling paint – it looked as if it had been olive green once, but had declined to grey – La thought, as might anybody who had made a precipitate move, *What have I done?* The answer was simple, of course; she had left London behind her, city and friends, without thinking of the implications. In a sense that was what she wanted: even if she still thought of Richard, and, curiously, still missed him – his absence was an ache within her – she did not wish to live in the physical space that her ruined marriage had occupied, and had turned her back on that. Now that the reality was upon her, she thought of ways in which what she had done might seem less extreme. Suffolk was not the end of the world, nor was London the world's centre, no matter that a good number of its inhabitants thought just that. The village, in fact, was only eighty miles from London – a couple of hours on the train and then not much more than twenty minutes in a car along these winding lanes. In three hours she could be back in town meeting her friends for lunch in some hotel, playing bridge; she could be back on the tennis court; it was not as if she had gone to Australia. But it might have been, as she stood there at the doorway, the taxi-driver helpfully bringing her suitcases down the path.

'The Stones never came here very much,' he said, huffing from the exertion of carrying La's heavy luggage. 'Only once or twice, I think, after the old lady died. So how long are you going to be staying?'

How long was she going to be staying? Forever? Until she was seventy, or even beyond? She would be seventy in 1981, but she could imagine neither being that age nor what the world would be like in 1981. 'I'm going to live here,' she said quietly. 'Permanently.'

The driver put down a case and extracted a handkerchief from his pocket. 'You'll be needing my services then,' he said. 'Getting you to the station. Into Bury. That sort of thing. I'm always available.'

'Thank you. But I think I shall buy a car.' She had not thought about it before this, but it was obvious now that this was what she would have to do. She would buy a small car – one of those open-topped ones that looked such fun in the summer, but that could be battened down for the winter.

'A car? I can sell you a car,' said the driver. 'I have the local garage, you see. I have reliable cars for sale.'

'Thank you.'

'So what sort do you want?'

'An open-topped one.'

The driver smiled. 'I have just the car for you. Just the job. I'll bring her round.'

She wondered whether this was the way things were done in the country. She had not asked about the colour, which was more important to her than any mechanical detail. But it seemed reasonable enough; she was going to live here, among these people, and she should give them such custom as she could. There would be other local tradesmen, no doubt, who would see her as a new customer; a butcher, grocers, fishmongers; a roofer perhaps to attend to the tiles. It was very quiet, she thought, and there would not be much doing by way of commerce.

The driver went off for the last of her suitcases and brought them back to her. She reached for her purse to pay him, but he laid a hand on her forearm. 'No, that won't be necessary. Not if we're going to be doing business together.'

'That would never happen in London,' she said, laughing. She was touched by his gesture.

'Never been there,' said the driver. 'No need for me to put up with their unfriendly ways.'

La, momentarily taken aback, glanced at him, and then looked away. Of course there were people in the country who had never been to London; she should not be surprised by that. But where, she wondered, did his world end? At Newmarket? Or Cambridge perhaps?

'I've been to Ipswich,' he said, as if he had guessed the question that had taken shape in her mind. 'And Norwich, once.'

'You don't need to go to London,' she said quickly. 'I'm pleased to be away from it, as you can see.'

If he had taken offence, it did not show. 'London's all right for them that wants to live on top of one another,' he said. 'But if you like a bit of sky . . .' he pointed up, 'then Suffolk's your place.'

She fumbled with the key that her father-in-law had given her.

'Rain,' said the driver, taking the key from her. 'Rain gets into a lock and brings on rust. She'll ease up once you're using her. A spot of oil, too – that helps.'

He pulled the door towards him and twisted the key in the lock at the same time. The door opened and at that moment, in headlong flight towards the light, a bird flew past them, out into the air. La screamed; the driver turned round and looked at the disappearing bird. 'A magpie,' he said. 'They get down the chimney. That one can't have been trapped for long – still plenty of energy in him.'

They entered the hall. There were white bird droppings like lime on the floorboards.

La looked about her. 'Poor bird. What a nightmare to be imprisoned.'

'Put a cowl on the chimney,' said the driver. He thought of further perils. 'And you could get bats, you know. They like to get in under the eaves; swoop around at night. Dive-bomb you.'

La wondered whether he was trying to scare her, as country people might do with somebody from the city. She thought she would tell him. 'I grew up in the country,' she said. 'In Surrey. I know about bats.'

He put a suitcase down and went out to collect another from just outside the door. Once he had brought them all in, he took a step back and smiled at her. 'People will help you,' he said. 'I expect that they'll already know you're here. Mrs Agg at the farm. Mrs Wilson in the village. They'll be round soon enough.'

He left, promising to bring the car a few days later – after he had attended to one or two little problems it had. 'Nothing big, mind. Small things. Spark plugs and the like.'

Alone, she closed the front door behind her. It was summer, and yet the air inside had that coldness that one finds in a house that has been shut up too long and not lived in; coldness and dankness. But these would be dispelled once the windows were open. The air outside had been warm and scented with grass, a sweet scent that would quickly pervade the house once it was admitted.

She moved through the hall, a square room on each side of which there were closed doors, panelled and painted in the same stark white that had been used on the walls. At the far end of the hall a not-quite-straight corridor led off to the back of the house; light, a bright square of it, flooded through a window at the end of the corridor, yellow as butter. A pane was missing – she could see that from where she stood – that was what had provided ingress for the magpie, and could be more easily remedied than the lack of a cowl on the chimney.

La opened the door to her left. Richard's mother had told her about the sitting room, that it enjoyed the sun in the mornings and that they had taken breakfast in there as the kitchen, on the other side of the house, was cold until the late afternoon. Now, at midday, the sitting room seemed warmer than the rest of the house.

'It's not a grand place,' she had been warned by her mother-in-law. 'It's a farm house, really, nothing more, but over the years it has been added to. There's some panelling – of a sort – in the sitting room. That's its sole distinction, I'm afraid.'

She saw the panelling, wainscot high, left unpainted; it had been faded by the sun, which, through the unusually large windows, must have reached into every corner of the room; now the wood was almost white, all colour drained from it. There was an attempt at a cornice on the ceiling, a strip of plaster relief running round the room, and, in the centre, a half-hearted plaster-rose from which the ceiling light descended. The floor was made of broad oak-boards, faded and uneven, but with a sheen to them, as if polish had been applied. A large russet-coloured carpet, almost perfectly square, of the sort that La's parents called a Turkey, dominated the centre of the room. Armchairs, shrouded with dust sheets, had been moved against the walls, watched over by paintings of country subjects: a still-life of a hare and pheasant shot for the pot, a watercolour of a flat landscape under banks of clouds, a hunting print of a line of horses launching themselves over a hedgerow.

La stood quite still. It was a room without life, like one of those Dutch interiors from which the people had disappeared, paintings of emptiness. She moved to a window and looked out. This was her first glimpse of the garden, as it was concealed from the front and one could only guess at what lay behind the house. Somebody had cut the lawn – quite recently, it seemed, which would explain the smell of grass on the air outside, that sweet, promising scent. At the end of the lawn, a line of plane trees interspersed with chestnuts marched several hundred yards to a low stone wall, and beyond the trees were fields. It was a warm day, and there was a slight haze hanging above the horizon, a smudge of blue that could mislead one into thinking that there were hills. London was far away already; how quickly would one forget in a place like this, she wondered. Would her own world draw in just as the driver's had? Suddenly it seemed perfectly possible that it might; that this was precisely the sort of place where one could cocoon oneself in a tiny world and forget about one's previous life.

She turned away from the window and continued her exploration of the house. Half-way down the corridor a steep wooden staircase, painted light grey, ascended to the floor above. La climbed this, the boards of the stair creaking beneath her, the only sound in the house. She looked into the bedrooms; there was a well-stocked linen cupboard, she had been told, but the beds were bare, the mattresses stripped of sheets. There was a bathroom with a claw-foot iron tub and a generous, shell-shaped porcelain basin. She turned a tap and water flowed, brown for the first few seconds, and then clear. A magazine, *Country Life,* a year old, lay on top of a laundry basket; a large cake of soap, cracked and ancient, had been left in a small china soap-dish by the side of the bath.

She went out onto the landing, and that was where she was standing when she heard the sound of somebody downstairs, the sound of feet upon the floorboards of the corridor.

Five

Mrs Agg explained that she had come into the house because she had seen the front door open.

'I didn't mean to give you a fright,' she said. 'I saw you coming, see. And I thought that'll be the woman from London. Mrs S wrote to me to tell me.'

Mrs S, thought La. Mrs S and her husband, Mr S and their son, R . . .

'I had a bit of a fright,' she said. 'But not much. I didn't realise that I'd left the door open.'

'Oh, it was closed. But not locked. We don't lock our doors in the country.'

La wondered whether there was reproach in the tone of voice, but decided that it was more a weariness at having to make what might be the first of many explanations. She felt a momentary resentment; she was not going to be condescended to because she came from London.

'Actually, I was brought up in the country myself,' said La. 'Surrey.'

Mrs Agg shook her head vehemently – with the air of one to whom the idea of visiting Surrey was anathema. Then they looked at one another in appraising silence. La saw a woman in her fifties somewhere, a thin face under greying hair pulled back into a bun, dark eyes. And Mrs Agg, for her part, saw a woman in her late twenties – much younger than she had expected – dressed in a London way, or what she thought they must be wearing in London. She glanced down at La's shoes; they would not last long in the mud. The soles would peel off; Mrs Agg had seen that before; people who came here and thought that they could wear London shoes; their soles peeled off quickly enough.

'I didn't tell you my name,' the older woman said. 'Glenys Agg.'

'And I'm La Stone.'

Mrs Agg frowned. 'La is that Lah, with an h? Or Lar, with an r?'

'La, with nothing. As in do-ray-me-fa-so.'

Mrs Agg looked puzzled. 'It's short for something, is it?'

La sighed. 'Lavender, I'm afraid.'

'No reason to be afraid of that,' said Mrs Agg. 'Plenty of lavender round here. And they could call you Lav, couldn't they, which would never do, would it?'

La wanted to talk about something other than names. She asked about the farm.

'It's on the other side of your place,' said Mrs Agg. 'Ingoldsby Farm. Ingoldsby was my husband's great uncle on his mother's side. His son died in the war, and so when old Ingoldsby himself passed on five years back we got the farm.'

La nodded towards the kitchen. She assumed there were chairs there and she could invite Mrs Agg to sit down.

'I can't stop,' said Mrs Agg. 'Not now. But I've brought you some things to tide you over. It's never easy moving into a new place. You never have any food in the house.'

La saw that there was a basket at Mrs Agg's feet. Her eye took in the contents: a few eggs, a handful of green beans, a loaf of bread wrapped in a thin muslin cloth; a small jar of butter; some tea. 'That's very thoughtful of you,' she said. 'I brought a few provisions with me, but it's never enough, is it?'

They went through to the kitchen and unpacked the basket. There was a meat-safe in the wall, a wooden cupboard that vented out through gauze into the open air outside. She put the bread and eggs in there, and placed the rest of the foodstuffs on the kitchen table.

Mrs Agg pointed to the range on the far side of the road. 'There's coal outside,' she said. 'I had them drop some by when they brought our load the other day. Two shillings' worth. You'll need to get the range going if you're going to have tea today. Do you know how to do it?'

La thought that her visitor already knew the answer. It was not the sort of thing one learned in London, she would think; nor in Surrey for that matter. But she did not want to admit, to Mrs Agg at least, that she had never fired up a range. 'I'll cope.'

Mrs Agg looked doubtful. 'If there's anything else you need, I'm at the farm. All the time.'

La thanked her, and the other woman left. She was curious to find out more, but had not felt that this was the time to ask. What was Mr Agg's name? Was there a post-bus to Bury? Where was the nearest butchers, and when was it open? There would be an opportunity for that later; there would be time for her to learn everything about this place in the days and months to come.

By herself again, she completed her exploration of the house, finding the linen cupboards and making a bed for herself in the bedroom at the back of the house, the airiest of the rooms she had found. The linen was clean, and smelled fresh, with small sachets of lavender laid upon it. Mrs Agg kept an eye on the house, she had been told, and cleaned it thoroughly every month. La thought of the broken pane and the magpie; the pane must have been recently broken, or Mrs Agg would have noticed it. How did a pane of glass break like that? Perhaps a bird had flown into it, or boys playing in the garden had thrown a stone.

She investigated the garden. In the summer afternoon the plane trees cast long shadows across the lawn and against one side of the house. An unruly hedge of elder bushes, twelve feet high or so, shielded the garden from the lane. The bushes were in flower, and she picked a head from one of them as she walked past. She could make elderflower wine, perhaps, or fry the flowers in sugar to make an old-fashioned sweet. Or simply weave elder branches about the kitchen door to ward off flies; her mother had sworn by that remedy.

She stood still for a moment and looked at her garden. Cutting the grass had given it a not altogether deserted look, but at all the edges it was unkempt. The lavender that Mrs Agg had mentioned was there, but had grown woody. What had been a vegetable patch was almost entirely overgrown by weeds, although La spotted a ridge of potato plants that had loyally persisted. She bent down to examine one of these and scrabbling in the earth beneath the foliage she retrieved a handful of small potatoes. She took these into the kitchen and dusted the earth from them; they would do for supper tonight, with the eggs that Mrs Agg had brought. My first night in my new home, she thought; my first night. And then, sitting down on one of the chairs in the kitchen, she looked at the ceiling and thought: *have I made a terrible mistake?*

There was a wireless in the sitting room, which she switched on after supper. There was still light in the evening sky, although it was now after nine o'clock. She turned on a table light, a single bulb under a cream-coloured shade. It provided a small pool of light, enough for comfort, but barely enough to read by. The wireless was comforting too, another presence in the house, and a familiar presence as well: the national service of the BBC. There was a literary discussion: Mr Isherwood and Mr Auden had returned from China the previous month. Mr Auden had written a number of poems and Mr Isherwood had kept a diary. Literary London was waiting with bated breath; in New York, *Harper's Bazaar* had already published a number of articles about their trip. Now people were wondering about the war that the Japanese had provoked with China. Was it true that normal life was going on in Shanghai even after the Japanese occupation? Mr Isherwood had recorded some observations, which were broadcast in full. 'You can buy anything in Shanghai,' he said. 'And life proceeds as it always did, in spite of the Japanese occupation.' Did you see brutality? 'We did. War is madness let loose. There is always brutality.'

Generalissimo Chiang Kai-shek? I gather that you met him. 'And Madame Chiang as well – we met both of them. We went to tea with Madame Chiang, actually, and she said to Wystan, "Please tell me, do poets like cake?" Auden replied: "Yes. Very much indeed." "Oh, I am very glad to hear it," Madame Chiang said. "I thought they preferred only spiritual food."'

La thought she heard the interviewer laugh, but only briefly.

She wondered how she would do if she went off somewhere, as Auden and Isherwood had done. She had known somebody who had gone to Spain, to drive an ambulance with the International Brigade, where he had witnessed a massacre by the Nationalists. Almost every adult male in a particular village had been shot, and the women and children had been made to watch. He had returned to England silent and withdrawn. His smile, which she remembered for its breadth and readiness, had disappeared, and now he looked away when you spoke to him. He never talked about it; no mention of the ambulance, nor the massacre, which had been reported by somebody else. He just nodded and said that he had been in Spain but that now he was back.

People were talking of another war, and had been doing so more fervently since the Austrian *Anschluss*. But La thought that war was unlikely, if not impossible. Rational men, meeting around a table, could surely never sanction something like that again. They all knew – they had seen the newsreel footage – of the sheer hell of the trenches; the pitiless carnage. How could anybody with any grip of their senses envisage doing something like that again? It was inconceivable, and Mr Chamberlain obviously understood that very well. But did Mr Hitler? What a buffoon that man was, thought La. With all his strutting and ridiculous bombast; an Austrian rabble-rouser pretending to be a statesman. Ridiculous.

If war came, then what would she do? There would be no point in going back to London, as she would have nowhere to stay and she would just be another mouth to feed. It would be better to remain in the country; to grow vegetables and contribute to the war effort in whatever other way she could. But it would not come: war was an abomination, a sickness of the mind: at the last moment people would surely pull back from something that brought with it a risk of their destruction. Or would they?

The voice on the radio caught her attention. It was another poet. 'War seems inevitable to me,' he was saying, 'because the monster of fascism can survive only if it has people to devour. There is no dealing with such a creed. To talk is a sign of weakness which will be pounced upon. To negotiate is to expose one's fear. The only hope for us is to become strong; for trade-unionists and workers to assert themselves and to make sure that the country allies itself with the great progressive forces of our modern world – and by that I mean the Soviet Union. Sooner or later the working people of Germany and Spain will rise up and defeat their oppressors. That's the way to avoid war. The dictators will fall at the hands of their own people.'

She went to bed. The sheets smelled strongly of lavender, a soporific smell; and she was tired from the trip, so sleep overtook her quickly. It was so quiet; that surprised her, as she was used to the constant background noise of London, the distant rumble of trains, the sound of traffic, the noise of millions of people breathing – even that must create a background of sound. Here there was nothing, just the occasional creaking of the house and a scurrying sound of mice or some other small creatures across the roof or in the attic above her head.

She awoke in the night, disoriented, and it took her a few seconds to remember where she was. She switched on her bedside lamp, and looked about her; her door was open – had she left it like that? She got out of bed and pushed it shut. She had locked the front door before she had turned in; would Mrs Agg censure her for that, she wondered, or was one meant to leave one's door open at night as well?

The following morning, La walked down to Mrs Agg's farm. Agg himself was not there, but she saw a man in the distance, in a field where sheep were kept, and that was Agg. Mrs Agg was happy enough to sell La a large packet of seed potatoes – 'Late-growing,' she said. 'You will still have time to plant these and to harvest them in the late autumn, before the ground becomes hard.' She paused. 'Why is a young person like you shutting herself away in that house? Sorry to ask.'

La thought for a moment before replying. 'My husband ran away with another woman, Mrs Agg. I was very unhappy. I felt that I wanted to get away.'

Mrs Agg nodded. 'I thought it was something like that. Any woman who's unhappy – look for the cause and it'll be a man.'

'So here I am,' said La.

La cleared a patch of vegetable garden. The long roots of the weeds yielded only under protest, clinging to the soil, and it was hard work. But by late afternoon she had two freshly-turned mounds of earth in which the potatoes could be planted. It was good soil; clay loam. I shall not starve, she thought. Whatever happens in the world, I shall not starve here in this quiet corner of England.

Six

A few days later, La drove to Bury in the car that she had bought for sixty-five pounds from the garage-man, Mr Granger. It was an Austin Seven, a small car painted in dark green with a hood that could be taken down in fine weather. La kept the hood on that day, as she was not sure how to operate the mechanism that released it; Mr Granger had shown her, but she had forgotten; there were levers which had to be pushed a particular way, this way or that, she could not remember. There was quite enough air, though, from the wound-down windows to give the feeling of being in the open.

La had some experience of driving, even if not a great deal. Richard had owned a car, which she had taken out from time to time when she went to play tennis in Richmond. She realised now that she had no idea what had happened to that car. Perhaps it had been left at the office, but nothing had been said, and she did not want to ask. Perhaps he had taken it on the boat with him to France; perhaps the Frenchwoman would be sitting in her seat – La's seat – and driving with Richard along the winding roads of Aquitaine; in her seat; with her husband. She put the thought out of her mind; if she allowed it to stay, then for the rest of the day it would be like a nagging pain, refusing to budge, always there. She would not let that happen to her, now that she had started this new life.

You can forget his car, she told herself, because you have your own car now. And you have your own life, here in Suffolk, with your own friends . . . But that is where the attempt at reassurance stumbled. There were no new friends; not yet. The only people she had met so far, apart from Mrs Agg, were Ethel, the woman who ran the village post office, and a man who had come out of the pub and lifted his hat to her in a show of elaborate courtesy; he had been drunk, she decided, but she had nodded curtly and had not stayed to hear him out. Mrs Agg was solicitous, yet she could hardly imagine herself developing a friendship with the farmer's wife. La was no snob, and did not care what drawer people were from – her mother's expression, and like many of the things said by mothers, alarmingly persistent in its resonance. The problem with Mrs Agg was that they had no interests in common, other than the cultivation of vegetables, perhaps; on which subject Mrs Agg had revealed her misgivings about the extent of La's knowledge. *I can grow potatoes*, La thought, through the mental equivalent of clenched teeth. *I know about these things. In Surrey we . . .* But she had never grown potatoes in Surrey, she had to admit. There may have been potatoes in the walled kitchen garden, but she had neither put them there nor nursed them to readiness. There had been a gardener who came three days a week; her involvement with potatoes had extended at this point merely to the eating of them; not that she could mention that to Mrs Agg, who would have simply had her prejudices confirmed by such a disclosure.

In due course, thought La, I shall receive invitations. These would not come from the villagers, who would not make a habit of entertaining, but from the larger houses in the vicinity. And there was always Bury, which was not too far away and which had the sort of population that one might expect to find in a prosperous market town: professional people, business people, teachers and so on. These were people with whom she would be able to discuss things, who read books and had views. And people of her own age, with a social life.

She drove into Bury and parked a short distance away from the Cornhill. It was market day, and produce stands stood in a colourful row along the side of the street. She walked past these, looking at the vegetables, the unpopular Flet cheeses, the bottled fruit. On impulse she bought a large ball of string – she had not seen any string when she went through the drawers in the kitchen – and it was something one always needed. Soap, a roll of white bandage for domestic injuries, two large boxes of cook's matches; these were all cheaper here, and she would need them. She found a stall selling books, and could not resist a book on the growing of roses. She noticed that the author's name was Thorn, and pointed this out to the stall-holder, who glanced at the cover, nodded and said, 'Terry Thorn. Big rose man over in Ipswich.'

'I suppose he had to write books about roses,' said La. 'It was inevitable. Mr Thorn.'

The stall-holder nodded. 'Knew so much about roses that he had to put pen to paper.'

Then she found a grocery store and went through the list of supplies she had written out the day before. We haven't seen you before, madam; would you like to establish an account? Of course. Thank you. An account gave her a feeling of belonging; it was a small part of her new identity.

The grocer's boy carried her purchases to the car. He whistled as he walked behind her, but stopped when La turned round to smile at him.

'Don't stop. I know that tune.'

'I wasn't thinking.'

'Whistling's nice. Cheerful. You must be happy.'

'I can't complain.'

Suddenly she felt that she wanted to ask him something. 'How old are you?'

He looked away. 'Sixteen. Seventeen in December.'

She was walking beside him now, not ahead. 'And do you think there's going to be a war?'

He was surprised by her question. He's just a boy, she thought.

'Maybe,' he said. 'Yes, maybe. Mr Evans in the shop says that there's going to be a war very soon. A couple of weeks, he thinks. He says that old Hitler has wanted it for years to make up for the fact that they lost last time. He says that if there is one, then he'll have to get a girl to do my job as I'll have to go off and fight. That's what he says. My Mam says different, though.'

She looked at him, and saw him, in her mind, in a uniform. It would be too big for him; too big around the shoulders.

'And what do you think about that? Going off to fight?'

He shrugged, and shifted the weight of the box of groceries in his arms. 'I don't know. If the other lads go, then I'll go. I don't mind. Better than sitting around here. Might meet some girls, you know, if I go somewhere else. Better than the girls round here, most likely.'

She wanted to say to him that one did not join the army to meet girls, but did not. Instead, she said, 'Have you ever read any poetry?'

The boy shook his head, and gave her a sideways look. 'No. I can't say I have.'

She had been thinking of Dr Price, her tutor, who had introduced her to the work of Wilfred Owen. She wanted to talk about Owen now, suddenly, rather urgently, but could not, of course, to this boy, even if he was exactly the sort of boy that Owen wrote about; gentle, rather passive boys from places like this, innocents who had been tossed so heartlessly into veils of gunfire: *The shrill demented choirs of wailing shells; And bugles calling for them from sad shires.*

The boy muttered, 'What did you say?'

She had not been aware of saying anything; but she had. 'I was thinking about how horrible war is.'

'Is it?'

'I'm afraid it is. That's why I hope that there isn't going to be one after all.'

It was when La returned to the house after this trip to Bury that she noticed it. She was unpacking her purchases in the kitchen – the string, the groceries, the book on roses – laying everything out at one end of the scrubbed-pine table when she saw that the tea caddy had been moved. It was not something, perhaps, that she would normally have paid much attention to, but she remembered very clearly placing it back on the lowest of the kitchen shelves, just above the hook on which the largest of her saucepans was hung. She remembered that because she had spotted a patch of grease on the bottom of the large saucepan and had dabbed at it with a kitchen towel. She had thought that she should wash the saucepan again, but had decided to leave it, and had given the tea caddy a quick wipe with the towel. She had not moved it; it had been there on the shelf, and now it was on the shelf above that.

Of course she doubted her recollection. Perhaps she had lifted the caddy from its place to dust it and had then replaced it on the shelf above. But asking herself this question she answered it immediately: she had not done that. She simply had not done that.

She crossed the room and took down the tea caddy from the shelf. Reaching for it gave her another reason to be sure; she could not reach the higher shelf unless she stood on a stool. She stopped, her hand barely around the caddy above her head. Suddenly she was frightened. She stepped down off the stool and spun round; she did not want her back turned to the open kitchen door, and the corridor beyond it. Somebody had been in her kitchen and had moved the tea caddy. That person, whoever it was, could still be in the house.

She left the kitchen and made her way slowly down the corridor towards the front of the house. Once in the hall, she pushed the sitting-room door open and peered in. There was nobody. Nor was there anybody in any of the other rooms; she went into each of them, her heart racing with anxiety, but she saw nothing untoward.

She returned to the kitchen, where she riddled the cooking range before feeding in fresh coal. Then she put on the kettle and sat down at the kitchen table. She picked up the newly-acquired ball of string and fiddled with it briefly, thinking. She could not remember whether she had locked the back door on leaving for Bury; and if she had locked it, then had she locked the front door as well? She thought that she had, but she could not be sure.

She rehearsed the possibilities in her mind. If she had locked up, the only other person who could have been in the house was Mrs Agg. She still had the key that she had used when she had been looking after the house, and La had suggested that she keep it. 'I'll need somebody to have a key in case I lock myself out,' she had said. 'Will you hold on to it?'

Mrs Agg had agreed, but had not used it, as far as La knew. In fact, after their first encounter, when Mrs Agg had come into the house unannounced, she had only come to the house once or twice, and on each occasion had made a point of knocking. It was possible, she supposed, that the farmer's wife had taken it upon herself to come into the house, but it seemed unlikely.

La decided to speak to her. She left the house, locking the back door carefully this time, and walked down the lane to Ingoldsby Farm. Mrs Agg was in the yard, gathering washing from the line, and waved to La as she saw her approaching.

'I saw your new car,' she called as La crossed the yard towards her. 'It's a very nice little car.'

'Thank you. Mr Granger . . .'

'He knows his cars,' said Mrs Agg. 'If Agg bought a car it would be from Mr Granger. But he hasn't.'

'I'll run you anywhere in mine,' said La. 'Just let me know.'

La was standing before her now, watching the other woman wiping her hands on her apron. 'Mrs Agg,' she began. 'Thank you for keeping an eye on the house.'

Mrs Agg looked up in surprise. 'Don't do much,' she mumbled; she had wooden washing pegs in her mouth. She removed the pegs before continuing, tucking them into the pocket of her apron. 'When I walk past, of course, I cast an eye to make sure you're not on fire, or something awful like that. Apart from that, don't do anything as I can see.'

La caught her breath. 'But I thought that you dropped in today.'

Mrs Agg shook her head. 'No. I've been busy here all the time. I didn't drop in.'

La could tell that she was telling the truth. 'Oh well . . .'

Mrs Agg looked at her expectantly, and then changed the subject. Would La fancy a couple of duck eggs? Not everyone liked duck eggs, of course; one of Mrs Agg's relatives was sick if she ate anything with duck egg in it. Just the yolks, though; the whites did not have that effect.

She went to fetch the duck eggs from the kitchen and handed them over to La; pale blue things, larger than hen's eggs, fragile, warm to the touch. La carried them back to the house, one in each hand, gingerly. But her mind was on other things. When she got back, she laid the duck eggs down on a clump of grass outside the kitchen and reached into her pocket for the key to the door.

She would not need it. The door had been forced, from the inside, the split wood of the frame sticking up in splinters, like small pieces of straw.

Seven

The policeman lived in a neighbouring village, in a house behind a small sign saying *Police House*. He heard La out on the doorstep, raising an eyebrow when she explained that it looked as if the door had been forced from within.

'Very unlikely,' he said. 'Don't you think? People break into houses, not out of them, at least in my experience.'

La looked at the man standing in front of her, a tall, well-built man with sandy-coloured hair and a bemused expression. She wondered whether she had misinterpreted the evidence. But the wood had been splintered on the outside; if you pushed on the door from the outside, it would have broken on the inner part of the jamb.

The policeman frowned. 'Which way does the door swing? Out or in?'

La thought for a moment. She could not answer, and the policeman's frown became a tolerant smile. 'You see? Sometimes things look black and they're really white. And the other way round.' He paused, watching the effect of his remark on her. He was one of those men who treated women with well-meaning condescension, thought La. She had encountered them first in Cambridge, amongst the undergraduates who were the products of all-boys schools, whose only contact with women had been with their mothers, or domestic staff. And there had been college fellows and professors, too, who had taken the same approach, and appeared vaguely irritated that the times required of them to engage intellectually with women.

There was a silence. It made more sense for the door to have been forced from outside; otherwise ... the thought appalled her. If it had been forced from inside that would have been because she had locked somebody up in the house when she had gone to see Mrs Agg. So the intruder, the person who had moved the tea caddy, would have been hiding in the house and then, finding himself locked in, would have had to force the door to get out.

'I shall come and take a look,' said the policeman. 'I'd be obliged if you would take me in your car. Otherwise I should have to ride my bike and that would take a little while.'

'Of course.'

In the car, La asked him whether there had been burglaries in the district. 'I can count on the fingers of this hand,' he said, raising his right hand, 'the number of burglaries we've had in the last eight years, since I came to this job. And most of those were carried out by Ed Stanton over at Stradishall.' He gazed out of the window and laughed; he was relaxed now in her company, and La was warming to him.

'Ed left the district after the last one,' the policeman went on. 'He was roughed up by the victim's son, who happened to be a boxer. That sorted him out. That, and his missus giving him his marching orders. Burglars are usually cowards, in my experience. Say 'boo' to them and they turn and run. That's where women go wrong, in my view.'

La was puzzled. 'How do women go wrong?'

The policeman looked straight ahead at the road. They were almost there, and perhaps, thought La, it was the wrong time to get involved in a debate about what women did or did not do; men thought they knew, but how strange that their view of what women did was often so different from the view held by women, who did it. He continued, 'Burglars are scared of people who aren't scared of them. That's human nature, isn't it? But if you're scared of burglars, then they sense it, like animals do. You know how a dog will push its luck if it can tell that a person is frightened of it? Have you seen that?'

La nodded. They were on the edge of her village now, and she slowed the Austin down.

'Well,' said the policeman, 'if women stood up to burglars, then they'd back down. Scarper. Burglars have mothers, you see. No burglar likes getting a tongue-lashing from his mum.'

She had to laugh, and he laughed too. Then, in a few moments, they arrived, and La pulled the car off the road onto the drive. The gravel was vocal underneath the tyres of the car, a crunching sound, like waves breaking, thought La.

'So this is where you live,' said the policeman. 'Some people by the name of Stone own this place, I understand.'

'My husband's parents,' La began. She could tell, as she spoke, what he was thinking. 'He lives in France now, my husband. It's just me here. I'm Mrs Stone too.'

'Ah,' said the policeman. Then, as the car stopped, 'By the way, I never even told you my name. It's Brown, but everybody around here calls me by my Christian name and my surname together, Percy Brown. You can too, if you like.'

'Everybody calls me La,' said La, although nobody in the village, she realised, called her anything. Mrs Agg knew her name, but had not used it, as far as she could recall. If anybody else referred to her – and they must have said something among themselves, even if only to note her arrival – then they must have called her something else. *That woman*, perhaps, or *that woman who lives by herself*. That, she thought, was what she was to them anyway.

La showed Percy Brown the door, which she had shut and locked before fetching him. He opened it, and as she did so more splinters came away.

'You see,' she said. 'It looks as if it's been pushed from the inside.' She was less sure, though, and the doubt showed in her voice.

Percy Brown made a non-committal noise and bent down to examine the door. He was in his shirt-sleeves, and La noticed sweat-stained patches under his arms; it had been a hot afternoon and these were now damp. There was something very masculine about him, she thought; he was beefy; he was like a bull.

He straightened up and ran his finger down the inside of the jamb. 'Yes,' he said. 'Here, and . . . and here.'

La peered at the place where his fingers had stopped.

'You see?' he said. 'Can you see the marks? That's where they've prised at the door. A screwdriver, maybe. Something of the sort.'

'From the inside?'

Percy Brown sniffed. 'Looks like it.'

*   *   *

She made him a cup of tea and they sat together at the kitchen table. He drummed his fingers lightly on the surface, which irritated her. He noticed the direction of her gaze and checked himself.

'Sorry,' he said. 'Mrs Brown says that's my worst habit. But it helps me to think.'

'I don't mind,' said La. She did. 'And I don't want to stop you thinking.' She did not.

He leaned back in his chair and folded his hands across his stomach. 'Let's go over this again. You went to Bury and may or may not have left one of your doors unlocked. Correct?'

'Yes. I think I locked up, but maybe I didn't. I don't know.' She was aware that she was worrying away at the edge of a table napkin that she had left on the table, pulling at the threads. 'My neighbour says that nobody locks their doors round here.'

Percy Brown nodded. 'Nor they don't. And most of the time that's fine. But let's assume that you didn't lock up. If somebody came in, then he would have had to do so while you was ... you were in Bury. Then you came back and noticed that somebody had interfered with things in the kitchen. The business with the tea caddy.'

La, who was sitting facing the window, looked beyond Percy Brown's shoulder into the garden outside. She had left a long-sleeved blouse on the line, and its arms were flapping in the breeze. One of the wind-filled arms came into view at the edge of the window performing a frantic piece of semaphore that caught her eye and held it for a moment while Percy Brown drew breath. He had more to say.

'So,' he continued. 'That means that the intruder was probably in the house when you searched. You must have walked right past him. Not a nice thought, Mrs . . .'

'Stone. La.'

'Not a nice thought, Mrs Stone, is it? That worries me, you know.'

La was silent. She had wanted reassurance; she had even hoped that he might come up with some explanation, but instead she was receiving what amounted to a warning. She waited for him to say something. He looked at her, and unfolded his hands.

'Sometimes we get gypsies,' he said. 'They camp down by Foster's Fields, a few miles away. They can be trouble, as you'll know. Stealing. Even theft of livestock. Sheep aren't safe when they're around. They end up inside a gypsy belly pretty smartly.' He paused. 'But they don't go in for housebreaking. That's not really their style. They're outside thieves, that bunch.'

She felt that she had to say something. 'Not gypsies?'

'I don't think so.'

'So?'

'I think I'll just have to report this as an unknown intruder. We get cases like that. Somebody sees a door left open and goes into a house to take a look round, to see if there's anything that can be easily taken. We call them opportunistic thieves. But what I don't like about this is the fact that he was fiddling. Fiddling with the tea, of all things. That tells me something.'

She waited. He was looking at her now, with an eyebrow slightly raised; the look of an avuncular older man about to issue a warning.

'What does it tell you, Mr Brown?'

He looked away for a moment – to examine his fingernails. Then he folded his hands again. 'It tells me that he might be interested in you. If people are snooping around a house and nothing's stolen, then it sometimes means that somebody has too close an interest in another person. Watching them, so to speak.'

Eight

That night, or at least the earlier part of that night, was difficult. La left it as late as possible before she went upstairs to bed. She switched on all the lights downstairs, and turned the wireless up as high as she could. She chose Radio Normandie, which was playing dance music. There was a cheerfulness about that, an optimism, which was what she wanted. When she went from the sitting room into the kitchen, the sound of the radio followed her. From the kitchen it sounded almost as if somebody was having a party at the other end of the house; all that was missing was the hum of voices. Perhaps she would have a party some time; but where, she suddenly thought, would the guests come from? Dr Price might be invited over from Cambridge – it was not too far away. But then she did not like men to be at parties, whereas La did; so that would not work. Perhaps Mr Thorn, the author of the book on roses. If he lived in Ipswich, he might be able to motor over. She stopped herself; there could be no party for a long time yet.

There was no curtain in the kitchen, and so when she stood by the sink, filling the kettle, she was looking out upon darkness. Suddenly she noticed a shape a few feet into the dark, at the limits of the light that came from the window. She gave a start, putting the kettle down quickly, spilling water from the spout. But then she realised what it was, and her heart, which had raced, resumed its proper rhythm. The long-sleeved blouse she had seen earlier in the day was still hanging on the line; she had meant to retrieve it, but had forgotten to do so.

She leaned forward towards the glass pane of the window and looked out again. There was the shape of the elder edge and the trees black against the night sky. There was very little moon – just a sliver – and no other illumination. The Aggs' farmhouse could not be seen from that vantage point so there was not even a light from that. They would have switched everything off by now, anyway. Farming people went to bed early, to be able to rise at dawn, when there was work to be done.

La took a deep breath. If I am to live here, she thought, then I cannot let myself be frightened by emptiness and isolation. I shall have to confront my fear.

She moved towards the door and opened it, trying not to look at the signs of its earlier forcing. She did not wish to be reminded of her conversation earlier that day with Percy Brown – a conversation that had ended with his concluding that there was very little that he could do about her break-in. Now she took a few steps into the dark, and began to remove the wooden pegs that kept the blouse on the line. The garment was dry, and had the fresh smell of cotton that has been left out in the fresh country air, something that her clothing never had in London. Clothing left out in the garden there came in slightly grey, with that vaguely stale smell that could linger in the atmosphere for days when the winds were sluggish.

She held the cotton of the blouse against her cheeks, and breathed in. She looked about her, her eyes gradually becoming accustomed to the dark. The shapes became more defined now; the woody lavender emerged, the line of box, the large pieris at the edge of the lawn. She took a few steps deeper into the darkness, looking up as she did so, up at the stars, fields of them, it seemed, stretching above in the chambered sky above. As a girl she had known the names and position of the constellations, and some of these were still lodged in memory: Ursa Major, Andromeda, Cassiopeia. She would renew her acquaintance with them now that she was here in a place where the sky was not spoiled by light.

Suddenly she thought of Richard. She still thought of him every day, but for shorter periods now; he was still there, a stubborn presence, like a scar. Now, at this moment, she missed him sorely. She would give anything, she thought, to have him here beside her; to be with him right now, under this sky, in this place. Without him she had nobody to share this with; the experience was half what it could be.

She put the thought out of her mind. Shortly after Richard had left, a friend in London, to whom the same thing had happened – at the hands of a charming womaniser – had said to her that the trick was to forget the man. 'If they're not there, then we feel much better, you know. So banish him.'

'But how? How do you stop thinking of somebody when they keep coming back to you? When that person is the only person you want to think about?'

'You do what monks do when they think about women. You

train yourself to think of something else. In their case, the Holy Ghost, I suppose. Or the Devil, I suppose, if they wish to frighten themselves.' She made a face, which indicated that she did not believe in the Devil.

She had decided to do that; every time he came to mind, she would think of something else, of something very far from Richard. Dr Price, perhaps, her Cambridge tutor, about whose person there was not the faintest whiff of sulphur, but who could stand in for the Devil. She conjured up an image of Dr Price, even though her old tutor was no Old English expert, expounding to her on *Beowulf* in a drowsy supervision, neither of them enjoying the experience, both wanting to talk about Eliot, who was much more to the point than any Scandinavian hero. The dissonance between her memories and *Beowulf* was sufficient to banish the thought of Richard. And now, out in the garden at night, she thought of *Beowulf*, and vaguely of Dr Price, and Richard was gone.

She walked round towards the front of the house, enjoying the cool evening air. The lawn stretched before her, a dark sward, beyond which the plane trees were a black expanse reaching up to the rather lighter sky. She decided to walk in the direction of the trees; the conquering of her fear made her feel almost giddy and for a few moments she felt as if she might break into song. Once on the lawn, she slipped off her shoes, and felt the grass soft beneath her feet. Somewhere in the distance an owl cried, a sharp sound that she remembered from her childhood; there had been owls in the barn beside the house in Surrey and they were forever screeching.

She reached the plane trees and stood beneath them for a couple of minutes, relishing the sound of their leaves in the slight breeze that had blown up. Within moments the breeze dropped and the trees were silent again. A leaf dropped, and touched her gently on the cheek as it fell, like the wing of a tiny bird.

Then she saw the movement. A dark shape on the other side of the lawn detached itself from a shadow and moved, to become another dark shape closer to the house. La caught her breath and stared into the darkness, straining to make out the form of what she had seen. For a few moments it became even darker, though, as a wisp of cloud moved across what little moon there was; La thought she could make out the figure of a man, but then she realised that she was staring at the large wisteria she had been trimming earlier that day. To the right, then, and . . .

The man moved suddenly; just a few yards, but enough to make himself distinct against the light that was coming from corner of the large window in the sitting room; the curtains did not meet exactly, and light escaped, enough to silhouette the figure of a man.

'Boo!'

It came to her completely spontaneously; so quickly, in fact, that she was unaware of any decision to shout out. And afterwards, when the childish word had been uttered, so loudly that it seemed to fill the night, her breath was gone from her, and she gasped. And the gasp might have been at her own sheer effrontery, or her surprise at what happened next. She saw the man jerk, like a cut-out in a shadow-play, as if invisible strings holding him up had been jerked. Then she heard the thudding of his feet on the gravel as he tore along the path beside the house to make good his escape down the drive.

She stayed where she was for a few moments. She was shaking, but felt strangely elated, as if she had just run a race and reached the finish line far ahead of the other contestants. She thought she should be feeling frightened, but she did not; she had done exactly what Percy Brown had implied one should do to a burglar. You should say boo, and then, exactly as he had predicted, they would run, or scarper, as he put it. He had been talking of a metaphorical boo, but she had taken him at his word and done as advised, with the result that she now saw.

La crossed the lawn, back towards the house. Then, following the path round towards the back, she found herself on the drive. She felt no fear now as she walked down to the point where the drive joined the lane; the intruder would be well down the road now, heading back to wherever he came from; which must be, she thought, her village, or possibly the neighbouring village two miles away on the Bury road. That thought unnerved her; the idea that this sleepy little place could conceal somebody given to creeping round – and into – the houses of others was not a comfortable one. And yet criminals had to live somewhere; burglars had their neighbours, as indeed did murderers. Such people also had jobs, in many cases; worked alongside work-mates, stood or sat beside them in the pub; passed the time of day with others at the bus-stop. In spite of all this, of course, such people still did the things that they did: looked through windows, forced doors, and worse; even if it must have been more difficult for them than their city equivalents. In the city crime was anonymous; here it was personal.

From the edge of the drive, La noticed a light at Ingoldsby's farmhouse in the distance, in spite of the lateness of the hour. Agg was up, or Mrs Agg, perhaps, baking bread in the kitchen. She toyed with the idea of going over there right away, to tell her that that there was a prowler on the loose. Mrs Agg was proud of her Aylesbury ducks, and if the prowler was a thief – and he must be – then a duck would be a tempting target. But she decided not to go; she had no torch and the car was put away in the garage. She would go tomorrow.

She was at the back of the house now – the side that faced the lane – close to the kitchen door, from which she had left the house to go into the garden. She made her way to the door and pushed it open – or was it already open? She stopped. She tried to remember: had she left it ajar when she had gone into the garden, or had she closed it behind her? She closed her eyes. She had been at the kitchen window when she had seen the flapping of her blouse on the line; she had opened the door – she remembered the light from the door falling across the stone paving outside and then . . . then she had closed it because she remembered how dark it became when she did so. The paving had been dark. It had.

And now the door was slightly ajar and she did not have to turn the handle. This meant that the intruder had run round the side of the house and rather than running down the drive, as she had imagined he would do, he had gone into the house. She opened her eyes. She had forgotten that she had left a full kettle on the range and it was boiling vigorously now; its whistle had broken and it now let forth little more than a sigh. In the air there was the smell of onions; she had fried some onions earlier on to have with a piece of liver and there was lingering in the air that sweet, slightly pungent smell that took its time to fade. The thought occurred to her: he would have smelled that smell when he came in; he would have become party to that bit of her domestic life – her choice of dinner.

She hesitated. She wondered whether she should telephone Percy Brown and tell him that she suspected that the intruder was in the house again. But the policeman would probably be asleep by now, and surely he would ask her why she thought that there was somebody in the house. If she explained that the back door was slightly ajar, then he would be bound to think that she was imagining things. Doors can be blown open by the wind; doors could swing open entirely by themselves if not hung true. There were all sorts of reasons why doors could be thought to have been opened by somebody else – and one of these reasons was the overactive imagination of a woman adjusting to the business of living on her own.

She could not end up running off to Percy Brown every time she felt nervous, and anyway what had happened outside had shown her that the nervousness was on the other side. Yet, would a nervous man have run into the house? Hardly; what refuge would there be for him there?

La closed the door behind her, slammed it for the noise, and then locked it. Radio Normandie was still playing dance music at the other end of the house. She walked down the corridor and went into the sitting room to turn off the radio. Now there was silence, and she listened to that silence, which is never really complete; there were sounds. She heard her own breathing, and her heart, too, she imagined; you could hear such things in a quiet house, if you listened hard, and were close enough. Now, though, she switched off the lamps in the sitting room, but left the light in the corridor burning, both for reassurance and in order to light her way up the first part of the stairs.

Upstairs she again went from room to room, and found

nothing. She opened the door of a large wardrobe in the spare room and looked inside; she peered into the bathroom cupboard and behind curtains in her room. She said to herself: *there is nobody in this house, but me. I am not afraid.*

Nine

Such a bright light penetrated La's bedroom curtain, and so early, as it was mid-summer, and the sun was already above the horizon. The birds had been in full throat from five o'clock, asserting their territory to anybody who cared to listen, announcing the beginning of the rural day. La was not a late riser, but five was too early, even for her, and she lay under her blankets for another forty minutes or so, drifting in and out of sleep, before she eventually slipped out of bed and walked barefoot into the upstairs bathroom. Through the bathroom window, a rectangle of old glass with a vertical fault-line of trapped bubbles, La looked out over the fields on the other side of the lane. The field nearest the house had Agg's sheep in it, and a couple of his Jersey cows. The cows had been milked already, she could see; Mrs Agg had told her that Agg got up at four to do this, every day, month-in, month-out, and had been doing that since he was twelve. That was not uncommon in the country, where everybody seemed to have been in the same place, doing the same thing, for most of their lives. Percy Brown had told her that his father had been a policeman in a small town nearby, and the vicar, whom she had met briefly on the day after her arrival, had been born in a vicarage in Bury.

After breakfast La walked over to Ingoldsby Farm. Mrs Agg was shelling peas in the kitchen and called her in from outside.

'I could help you,' said La.

'You don't have to,' said Mrs Agg.

'I want to. Please let me.'

She sat down at the table alongside her neighbour.

'I had an intruder last night,' she said. 'In the garden. A man.'

Mrs Agg continued with her peas. She did not look up. 'I see.'

'Yes.' La had expected more of a reaction. Perhaps intruders did not count for much in the country.

Mrs Agg looked up briefly. 'A gypsy, I'd say. Foster's Fields. There's a gaggle of them down there.'

La remembered what Percy Brown had said. Gypsies were outside thieves. But surely not all of them; how could everybody be a thief?

'Yes,' Mrs Agg continued. 'They come round here on the look-out for anything not nailed to the ground. Like ducks.'

'So I shouldn't be worried,' said La.

Mrs Agg shook her head. 'Worried? Oh, no. They slink away pretty quickly if you shine a light at them. Like foxes, they are.' She paused. 'You weren't worried, were you? You can come over here if you're worried. I'll send Agg over with his shotgun.'

They lapsed into silence. La felt relieved; if what Mrs Agg said was true, and he had been a gypsy, then at least she could stop worrying about being watched. Gypsies stole, she had been told; they did not watch.

They worked for a further ten minutes. Mrs Agg was not one

for unnecessary conversation, and La assumed that there was nothing to be said. When they reached the end of the peas, the farmer's wife stood up and brushed at her apron. As she did so, a door behind her opened and a young man entered the room. He was about to say something, and had opened his mouth to do so, when he spotted La and stopped himself in surprise.

'This is my Lennie,' said Mrs Agg.

La looked up at the young man. He was tall – considerably taller than his father – and well-built. He had a shock of dark hair and one of those broad, country faces that could so easily become, as it did in this case, slightly bovine. It was not an intelligent face, La thought, nor a comfortable one; there was resentment in it, she thought. Things were not quite right for Lennie.

Lennie stared at La for a few moments before his gaze slipped away to the side. As this happened, though, Mrs Agg's eyes moved up and met La's briefly, as if in enquiry.

La forced a smile. 'Hallo, Lennie.'

'Yes,' he said. 'Yes.'

Mrs Agg dusted again at her apron. 'Those ewes, Lennie,' she said. 'Dad says he wants them moved over to the big pasture.'

Lennie nodded and moved off towards the back door. La noticed that his trousers, which were made of thick grey hodden, had patches of mud upon them, caked dry. On the sleeves of his shirt, which were rolled half way up the forearm, there were dark stains that looked like treacle: they basted something dark on the hooves of the sheep – she had seen it – to protect them from foot-rot; Stockholm Tar, she thought it was called. Some of this was on Lennie's shirt now. She noticed the skin on the back of his neck, just above the collar of the stained shirt; she saw that it was tanned by the sun, red-brown, leathery.

With Lennie out of the room, Mrs Agg glanced at her watch. 'I have to let the ducks out,' she said. 'We keep them in at night or the fox would get them.' She paused. 'Lennie is a worry to me, you know. But what mother doesn't worry?'

La felt a sudden surge of sympathy for Mrs Agg. 'I'm sure that he's . . .' she was unsure what to say, and she trailed away.

'He's twenty-three,' Mrs Agg went on. 'I sometimes wish that there was more for him to do round here, but there isn't, you know. They have a dance in the village hall from time to time, but Lennie's not very good with girls.'

'I'm sure that he'll find somebody.'

La saw the appreciation in the look she received from Mrs Agg. Nothing kind was ever said to her, thought La; she lived in a world of taciturn men, of hard work. 'I hope so. But not every girl is going to want to marry a farmer, these days. Girls have ideas about living in town. The comforts. Our life here . . .' She looked about her, at the kitchen, with the bowls of shelled peas, and the stack of wood beside the range; at the blackened griddle; at the rush mats on the floor with their frayed edges.

'Farmers' daughters?' asked La.

'Yes, that would be good. But Lennie, you see . . .' The sentence was not completed.

It then occurred to La that it was Lennie she had seen in the garden the previous evening. And it further occurred to her that Mrs Agg knew that, but could not bring herself to say as much. She was his mother, after all, and few mothers accept the truth about their sons, no matter how glaringly obvious that truth may be.

Over the weeks that followed, the second half of July, La saw no more of the intruder. She was now convinced that it had been

Lennie, and that Mrs Agg might by now have spoken to him. It was also possible that he had merely been curious, and that having met her in the farmhouse kitchen had somehow taken the mystery out of her presence. Whatever it was, she was not frightened of him; rather, she felt sorry for him, for this farm boy in whose life nothing had happened, who had probably never been to London, whose world began and ended with Ingoldsby Farm. She wondered what went on in his head. Did he listen to the news? Did he know where Germany was; who Hitler and Mussolini were? For such a young man, the arrival of a new neighbour must have been an event of tremendous import – enough to lure him into trying to find out more about her. Viewed in that way, Lennie was nothing to worry about. Indeed, when she saw him next she would try to reach out to him, to engage him in conversation, to find out more about his world.

On a Thursday morning, a young man rode a bicycle up La's drive. La spotted him from the kitchen. She saw him dismount, prop his bicycle against the sycamore sapling at the edge of the drive, and then take off his post office cap, wiping the sweat from his brow. It was warm work cycling in the summer heat and he must have come a fair distance – she had not seen him in the local post office. She dried her hands and went out to meet him.

'Mrs Stone?'

She nodded. He had extracted a telegram from his pocket and she was going over in her mind which of her elderly relatives could have died. Her father, now in a nursing home in Brighton, was frail, but July was not a month for bronchitis and its mortal harvesting. There was an aunt in York who had been ill, but who had written to her recently and claimed to have been feeling much better, had even spoken of coming down to say with her for a few days.

She took the telegram and signed the small notebook that the young man produced from another pocket. She searched his face for a sign; they knew what was in these telegrams, these men, but affected ignorance. They avoided smiling, she had been told, when the news was bad. His face was expressionless.

'Hot day, isn't it?' he remarked, looking away.

'Yes.' She thanked him and gave the notebook back. He nodded, and went back to his bicycle.

She had not expected it to be Richard, and the bearer of this news to be his father.

Regret Richard very ill in France. Shall come to see you late afternoon. Car from Bury. Will leave again following morning. Gerald.

She went back into the house and sat down on one of the kitchen chairs. Re-reading the telegram, she tried to extract further meaning from the sparse words. But she could not read anything more into the terse message: Richard was ill, his father was coming to see her and then leaving the next day. She thought: Richard is dying. And then she spoke the words aloud, 'Richard is dying.' Then, immediately, she told herself that this was not true. It was not something she could either believe or say. She had simply been mistaken. He was not dying.

She sat in silence. She watched the hands of the kitchen clock, an old railway timepiece rescued from a demolished waiting room somewhere, the minute-hand advancing jerkily around the dial. She closed her eyes and saw Richard standing before her, smiling as she remembered him smiling, the palms of his hands facing outwards in an ambiguous gesture somewhere between greeting and apology. Here I am, he said, without speaking. Here I am. Remember?

She went outside, intending to busy herself with some task that would take her mind off the wait for Gerald's arrival. She had planted several rows of spinach in her newly-cleared vegetable patch and now she bent down and began to pluck the weeds from either side of the spinach plants. She felt the moisture of the soil against her knees; she was ruining a good skirt, which was not made for such tasks, but she did not want to go back into the house to change. She plucked at the weeds and flung them to the side; she wept, and she saw a tear fall on the dry soil, a tiny drop caught in a fragile meniscus. Why should she cry for a man who had let her down so badly? Who loved another woman rather than her? Because women did; they wept for the men who misused them and betrayed them; and because La had wanted him, and still did; she wanted him with her, and because not an hour of her day went past, not an hour, but that she thought of him.

When Gerald arrived she was still in the garden.

'I'm a mess,' she said. 'Just look at me.'

He seemed surprised, almost irritated, that she should say this. Perhaps he had imagined that this would be no time for small talk. He frowned at her remark. 'There has been an accident,' he said. 'He was in the *caves* and a structure holding a barrel collapsed. A large piece of wood . . .'

She could not imagine the scene. How high was this structure? Was it a shelf? And where did the wood come from? It all seemed unlikely; an incomprehensible, foreign accident – unreal. *Caves*, barrels; these things did not *injure* people.

He looked down, and as he did so she reached forward and took his hand.

He swallowed. It was an effort to speak. 'A large piece of wood struck him on the head ... apparently. It was a bit of a fluke. Had he been standing a few inches to the side nobody would have been hurt.'

She pressed his hand. This was a father talking about a son, his only son. 'Oh, Gerald ...'

'They took him off to hospital, but apparently the injury to the head is terribly serious and he ... he's unconscious. The brain, you see. They don't think there's much hope of his pulling through. That's what they said to me.'

He looked up again and she saw the redness about his eyes. She moved forward and embraced him, feeling the large frame heave as he began to sob. She did not take in what he said; she had not heard the bit about not pulling through.

'My son. He was my boy. Just my boy.'

She hugged him. 'Yes. Yes.'

'I'm going to go first thing tomorrow. La Rochelle, I think. Winifred is with her sisters. They don't want her to make the trip. They say she couldn't take the strain, with her heart being what it is. I don't know.'

She hesitated, but only for a moment. 'Well, I'll come. I'll come with you.'

He said nothing, but she knew that this is what he wanted; this is why he had come to her.

'We'll go inside and I'll make you some tea. Then I shall get my things ready. Perhaps we could even leave tonight and try to make it to Dover so that we can cross first thing.'

He pulled away from her, gently, and took a handkerchief out of the top pocket of his jacket. He wiped at his eyes.

'I shouldn't,' he said. 'It doesn't make things any easier. I'm sorry.'

'But tears make things easier,' she said, taking his hand again. 'They do.'

She did not believe that; but at that moment, she believed nothing. She did not believe that Richard was seriously injured. He would come back. He would come back to her and they would be in London again, as they had been before all these unreal things purported to happen.

But when she woke up that night, and lay unmoving in her bed, the disorder of her thoughts dispelled itself. Richard was gravely ill in a French hospital. She was leaving the following morning to see him, to say good-bye. It was all very clear and unambiguous; quite unconfused.

Ten

The hospital was on the edge of Bordeaux, set in a large formal park where lines of cypress had been planted. The summer sun had turned the grass brown and now cast dark shadows beneath the trees. Here and there, in small bowers made by shrubs and pergolas, ambulatory patients in towelling dressing-gowns sat with one another or with relatives. Smoke rose from cigarettes; the sound of conversation; occasional laughter.

Gerald and La were dropped by the taxi driver at the front door. Above this door was a large frieze: a nurse, angular in stone, ministered to a man lying on a stretcher; on his chest, grasped in both hands, a crucifix. Immediately within was a reception hall, a large square room, at the side of which was a glass booth. A man sat behind a desk in this booth, a telephone beside him, a newspaper spread out before him.

Yes, he was expecting them. He gestured to a row of seats against the wall; if they would care to sit there for a few minutes, a doctor would be with them shortly. Gerald held his hat in his hands; he was fingering the brim in his nervousness. La touched his forearm in reassurance.

'They're being very kind, aren't they?' she whispered. Gerald nodded. 'We should sit down.'

They waited ten minutes or so before the doctor arrived. From time to time, La looked up, to catch the eye of the man in the booth. He smiled and pointed towards a door at the other end of the hall; the doctor would arrive, Madame should not be anxious. And then he was there, walking towards them, holding out a hand, initially towards Gerald and then, as if noticing her for the first time, to La.

La's French was rusty, but good enough for the present task. When she began to speak to him in his own language, the doctor visibly relaxed.

'I'm sorry that we meet in these difficult circumstances,' he said. 'I will take you and your father to his room.'

'I am the daughter-in-law,' said La. 'I am married to Monsieur Stone.'

The doctor appeared confused. 'But Madame . . .'

'We are in the process of divorcing one another,' said La. 'Now . . .' *La veuve*, she thought. *La veuve Stone.*

He understood. 'My apologies. I was not aware.'

'There is no reason why you should have known,' said La. She paused. 'Is . . . is Madame here?' How dare she, she thought. How dare she.

The doctor shook his head. 'She said that she would return later. I think she knew that you were coming.'

La looked at him. 'Can you tell us what the position is?'

'What does he say?' Gerald interjected.

'I'm asking him now. I'll tell you.'

The doctor invited them to sit down again. He drew up a chair and sat facing them. 'I'm afraid that the situation is very grave,' he began. 'The coma is profound and his breathing is becoming very laboured. I do not think that he will recover consciousness. I am very sorry to have to tell you this.'

Gerald leaned forward. 'No hope?' he said.

La looked down; Gerald knew.

'I can escort you to his room,' said the doctor. 'In these cases there are things that one might wish to say. Sometimes the patient hears, you know. I'm personally convinced of that. Sometimes he may be aware that somebody is there. You never know.'

They followed the doctor along a corridor, then up a staircase that turned back upon itself. There was a second corridor, with a lingering hospital smell, the odour of strong disinfectant. It caught the back of La's throat and made her stomach heave. Ammonia.

'Here,' said the doctor, gesturing to a half-open door. 'I will return later. There is no hurry.'

They stood in uncertainty until La pushed the door open and led the way in. For a few moments she did not look at the figure in the bed, at the head lying on the pillow, half-turned; she did not dare. Gerald moved past her to the top of the bed. He reached for Richard's hand, and held it. La felt the tears brim in her eyes and wiped them away. Now she looked at Richard's face. There was nothing wrong with him. He was simply sleeping; it was that deceptive. The ante-chamber of death, she thought; the sleep that will become death.

Gerald muttered something that she did not catch. She looked away, wondering whether she should leave him there alone with his son in this final farewell. And it was to be final; the doctor had made that clear.

'I'll wait outside,' she said. But Gerald shook his head and then bent down quickly, awkwardly, to kiss his son. Then he replaced the hand on the counterpane, slowly, with care, and turned away.

'I shall be in the corridor,' he whispered.

Alone with Richard, La stood beside the bed. The doctor's words were in her mind; there are things that one might wish to say. She looked at the bandage that was wound past the top part of Richard's head. There was a dressing underneath, to the side, and blood had seeped through, had turned black, a human crust. She looked at his eyelids; if there was consciousness within, if he was merely sleeping, there would be movements revealing the flickering of activity in the brain; the skin was taut, and still.

What should she say? What did one say to the dying in their beds? It's a fine day outside; we saw people on the benches, under the trees, enjoying the autumn sun. The trip from England was smooth; just a little rough in the early morning. I am enjoying living in Suffolk; you know the house, Richard. I have been working in the garden. I am lonely without you. So lonely. It is like an ache, right here – an ache.

Instead, she moved closer and sat on the edge of the bed, in silence. She took his hand, the hand that Gerald had held. It was warm to the touch, but it was as if there were no muscles controlling it, just passive flesh and bone. That hand had caressed her; that hand had placed a ring upon her finger. She remembered that now.

'I'm so sorry, Richard. I'm so sorry.'

A sound came from his lips. She looked up sharply, but it was just breathing; faint breathing, like the wind on a still day, an almost imperceptible movement of air, not enough to stir the leaves; a touch.

'I have come to tell you something,' she continued. 'Darling. My darling. I have come to tell you that I forgive you. I do.'

She waited for a response, but what did she expect? Some sign, perhaps, that he had heard, that he understood. But there was nothing; if there was any consciousness, somewhere in that sleeping mind, it was fixed on other things, dreams, flickers of light, remembered sounds, fragments of what had been.

She stood up. She felt as she had on the day, shortly after her thirteenth birthday, when she had been taken to the Bishop for confirmation. She thought that the experience of that oiled finger making the sign of the cross on her brow would change her; that she would feel herself transformed, filled with the inrush of some sort of spirit. But she had not; she had felt exactly the same as she always did, unchanged – and the world about her was as it ever was, prosaic, stubbornly ordinary. There had been no rush of the Holy Spirit, no roaring as of a waterfall, nothing; just the face of the Bishop who had cut himself shaving that morning, a nick on the chin, and had staunched the cut with styptic pencil – she could see the white mark it had made, like a small crust of salt.

Her words were unheard. But she had bestowed her forgiveness upon him, and as she turned and left the room, she thought: you can be forgiven without knowing it, and for the forgiver it does not matter that the recipient is unaware of what has happened; just as one may be loved by another without ever knowing it.

A different taxi-driver drove them back from the hospital. The one who had taken them there had been taciturn; this one was conversational.

'So you are going back to the harbour. The boat to England?

That is very wise. We are in greater danger here in France, as you no doubt know. You see that road over there, that one? That leads to the cavalry stables. They have turned the horses out of their stalls, you know, to accommodate the animals from the Paris Zoo. Did you know that? They have evacuated the animals from the zoo up in Paris because they know that the Germans will be coming. Or German aeroplanes, rather. Paris will be destroyed. They know that up there. They know that, and are trying to save the animals, even if they cannot save the people.'

'Your king is still there in London, I believe. Well, you tell *monsieur le roi* that if he had any sense he would be out of London. Anywhere. Go anywhere – anywhere – until the fighting is over. And get the animals out of London Zoo. You have a big zoo there, do you not? Send the animals over here; we shall look after them for you.'

In the taxi and at the harbour, Gerald seemed strangely composed. La looked at him anxiously as they boarded the ship. 'Are you sure that you are all right?' she enquired. 'Are you sure that you want to travel?'

He was adamant. He had accompanied her to France, and he would see her back safely. This was the way he was – stoic – and she knew that there was no point in her trying to persuade him she was capable of getting back by herself. He went to his cabin, but only after he had seen La to hers. Then, each alone in their different forms of sorrow, they began the crossing.

The following morning, shortly before twelve, the ship's engines suddenly stopped. They were four hours' steaming from Southampton, and the skies had clouded over slightly. The air now had a northerly smell to it, had become sharper, and the colour of the sea had changed, silver darkening into a grey-green;

the south, and the freedom it suggested, lay behind them. Some of the passengers came up on deck when the engines stopped, curious to see what had happened; a man overboard, perhaps, or one of the yachts they had seen earlier now in need of assistance. But the sea about was calm, and there was no other shipping to be seen. An off-duty member of the crew leaned over the railing, watching the wavelets below lap against the side of the ship; there was clearly no emergency.

The Captain's voice came over the loudspeakers that were affixed at points to the ship's superstructure. He spoke with the accent of Devon; a voice that struggled to sound grave, even now. 'This is the Captain speaking. I am very sorry to tell you: the radio room earlier today received a message from shore telling us the Prime Minister has addressed the nation. War has been declared on Germany. That is all we have heard.'

La had been standing on the aft deck. The wind was blowing straight on, and it carried the Captain's words quite clearly. After he had spoken, there was a short pause before the engines were started, and they got under way again. La stood where she was, near the starboard lifeboats. She put her hand against one of the boats. It felt sticky, from the salt spray that had blown against it; the stanchions holding it were rusted; she saw that. If somebody attacked them now, she wondered whether these ill-kept life-boats could be released. Somebody, somewhere, had to be the first civilian casualty. War. It was what people had feared for so long; it seemed unavoidable – like a brewing thunderstorm that one knew would engulf one. How was it that people had done nothing to stop it? Why had those who remembered the last time, and all its horrors, not risen up and shouted at the politicians, shook them, made them listen: *Never Again*? War.

She felt a cloying, leaden dread. Whatever happened – whether the war was businesslike and swift, or hopelessly drawn out – young men would lose their lives in their thousands, in their tens of thousands, their millions perhaps. It was happening; in a dreadful form of slow-motion it was happening. And this time, she feared, it would not be possible to hide away from it. This was a war that would involve them all. Gerald and his wife. The Aggs. Dr Price in her rooms in Cambridge. Her old neighbours in London. Herself. Now that war had been declared, they could come out into the open – those who would kill her; her, of all people; La. They could show their face.

For the rest of the voyage and on the train from Southampton, she did her best to comfort Gerald. His earlier composure failed him, and now he moved between silence and talkativeness, bringing up memories of Richard, sobbing occasionally, covering his face with his forearm, as if ashamed. 'You know what news we shall get when we return? You do know, don't you, La?'

'Sometimes people recover . . .'

Gerald shook his head. 'I don't think so.'

She travelled with him as far as London, where they said their farewells on a station platform within earshot of a newspaper man calling out, 'News from the war.'

'There can't be anything,' said Gerald. 'Not yet.'

'It won't last long,' said La. 'There'll be peace.' He was grieving already for his son, even if they had left him alive; she did not want him to have to worry about the war.

'No, there won't,' he said.

She returned to Suffolk. From the train window she saw that everything was normal; the crops were being brought in; a man stood on top of a haystack and lifted a fork of golden hay against the sky; boys leaned over bridges to watch the train go by; a couple held hands in the carriage, stole a kiss in a tunnel. In the taxi from the station, Mr Granger gave her his views on the situation.

'They'll sort Hitler out quickly enough,' he said. 'The War Office. The generals. They've never let us down.'

La was silent. 'They're very strong,' she said. 'The other side. They've been pouring money into armaments. Duff Cooper had to struggle to get anything to bring our forces up to date. Remember?'

'They'll be all right,' said Mr Granger. 'Look at the Spanish. Look at Napoleon. Look at the Kaiser. We dealt with them all. Sent them packing.'

He helped her with her luggage and then left. As she opened the front door, she saw the telegram that must have been sent shortly after she had left Gerald in London; he must have heard within minutes of his arrival. She knew what it would say, and so she did not open it, but placed it on the kitchen table, from where it stared at her, daring her to open it. She went into the dining room and wound up her gramophone. She chose Bach's *Mass in B Minor*, but only played one side of the first record. She moved to Mozart, because he had the greatest healing power. The music reminded her: love and loss were inextricably linked. This world was a world of suffering; music helped to make that suffering bearable. She listened intently, and then, as the record came to its end and the needle scraped against the last swirling grooves, she rose to her feet and lifted the arm of the gramophone and let the turntable spin round until its spring unwound completely and it stopped.

Part Two

Eleven

Now they had a war to fight, La wondered whether she should get back to London and volunteer. There were plenty of things for women to do; she had friends who were in the Wrens and the Women's Auxiliary Air Force; another drove an ambulance in Liverpool. Everybody, it seemed, could find war work – *should* find war work. She had wanted there to be peace – who did not? – but now the proponents of peace were discredited, or considered defeatist: Munich had been a shameful act of appeasement, people said. Few seemed to remember their relief at the time; the clarity of hindsight had almost obliterated memories of that.

In the February after the outbreak of war La visited a recruiting office in Cambridge, where she was interviewed by a carefully groomed major. The major's manner was formal; it was as if, thought La, he wanted to impress upon her the gravity of the work he was doing. This was military business; and so might a general sit at the board on which campaigns were plotted.

He moved the piece of paper in front of him on his metal desk. His hands, she noticed, were small. 'You are a widow, I see.'

She was not used to being called that, and hesitated a moment, as if the description did not apply to her. But she was a widow, of course; *la veuve Stone,* like a champagne heiress. What difference did it make to what she could do for the war effort? She had read that widows encountered social difficulties – balancing tables at dinner parties was widely said to be a problem – and thought: did the army and the air force have anything against widows? She studied the major. He was a man in his late forties, she thought; spruce and handsome in an asexual sort of way. Men in uniform may have interested some women, but had never meant anything to La. Uniforms destroyed individuality, she thought – that was what they were meant to do, after all – and characterless maleness was of no interest to her.

Did this major like women, she wondered; or was he one of those military men who prefer the company of other males? She met his eyes, and the retreat within gave her the answer.

The major picked up the piece of paper and then replaced it on the desk. 'I'm sorry,' he said. 'You have lost your husband very young.'

'Thank you. And, of course, being by myself now means that I can be flexible in the work I undertake.'

'Yes. Naturally.' He paused, then spoke; but not to La, more to himself, as if reviewing possibilities. 'We shall need more nurses.'

'I could do that.'

'You would have to train . . . and, well, they're taking single girls first. Young women. Eighteen or so.'

'I see.'

'I suppose that it's something to do with being able to train an eighteen-year-old more easily. Nurse training is almost like military training, I'm told. Very strict. Very demanding.'

La folded her hands. 'I have a degree,' she said. 'I am a grad-uate of the university.' She said this because she felt that she was every bit as trainable, surely, as an eighteen-year-old fresh out of school.

He lowered his eyes to the paper, and she realised that she had antagonised him. An unpromoted major in this unglamorous work, at the tail end of a career, would not have a degree. 'Which university?' he asked. He spoke in an offhand manner – as if he did not really expect, or want, an answer.

La looked out of the window. She could see the spires of King's from where she sat; if he turned, he could too.

'The one behind you,' she said, and smiled.

He did not seem to hear her answer. 'I note from your address that you live in the country, Mrs Stone.' He articulated his words carefully. 'We have any number of town girls, but how useful are they, do you think? We shall need people to work on farms. You will have noticed the introduction of rationing of bacon and butter. Sooner or later the authorities will have no alternative but to ration everything, I believe. We have to import so much . . .'

La was silent. War was not just the movement of troops, of tanks; it was the cutting of coal, the tilling of fields, the boxing of munitions; meetings like this one, boredom, long hours. She was scared of none of that.

'You think I should work on the land?'

The major nodded. 'Suffolk is a richer county than people imagine. I've always said that. Reasonable soil. Rich clay.' He reached into a drawer and took out a blue folder. 'I have a form here which I shall pass on to the Women's Land Army. They know where the need is. When spring comes, they will be crying out for people – especially if more young men join up.'

He gave her the form, and she filled it up, there and then, leaning on the uneven surface of his metal desk. He watched her as she wrote, but his eyes moved away when she looked up. She saw the buttons on the sleeve of his jacket, with their crown motif. The King's reach was a wide one – down to this officer's buttons. Having the symbol of another on one's buttons meant that the other owned you. A free man – a really free man – could not carry the symbol of another on his clothing.

She finished filling in the form, and gave it to the major. The section on experience was thin: she had written *gardening*, and left it at that. As she handed the form back to him, she asked, 'Do you think that we'll win this?'

She could see the effect of her question on him. He stiffened. 'Of course. There is no question about it.'

'I am not defeatist,' said La. 'I hate everything that Hitler stands for. I want us to win.'

He relaxed. 'I should hope so.'

'But I'm concerned. The ease with which the Germans have overtaken Poland . . .'

'Aided by their Russian allies,' interjected the major.

'Germany seems so strong. They have so many more tanks and planes than we do.'

The major looked at La pityingly. 'I wouldn't worry unduly about these things, Mrs Stone. We have the General Staff to do our worrying for us.' He paused. 'And as Voltaire said, *Il faut cultiver son jardin*. One must cultivate one's garden.'

He held her gaze.

It was not until April that La was contacted by an official of the Women's Land Army. They had heard she was available for work, and that she had offered to work without pay. They could arrange something, they said: a farmer in her area was having difficulty coping with his chickens after the young man who had been helping him had joined up. The farmer was elderly, and his arthritis was getting worse. It would not be heavy work – a few hours a day of feeding the birds and cleaning out the coops, and the farm could be reached by bicycle from her home. Would she do it? La telephoned the official and accepted.

She went to tell Mrs Agg. She was curious to find out if her neighbour knew the farmer for whom she would be working. She must do, she thought; Madder's Farm, where she would be working, was only about four miles away.

Mrs Agg smiled. 'He's a kind man,' she said. 'Henry Madder. And all his difficulties.'

La raised an eyebrow. 'His health? I heard that he had arthritis. Is there something else?'

She was talking to Mrs Agg on the small drying green outside the farmhouse kitchen. A basket of damp laundry was at Mrs Agg's feet, and she reached into this to extract a pair of trousers. They were Agg's trousers; La had seen him in them; grey trousers with large, roughly-sewn outside pockets.

'I wasn't talking about his health,' said Mrs Agg. 'Though it's true he has arthritis. I was talking about the business with his son, and with his wife after that. It was all because of the son that Helen Madder went, I think.'

La waited for her to explain. From the trousers, only half-wrung, fell a few small drops of water.

'It all started when Henry Madder ran over his young son,' said Mrs Agg. 'In his cart. He still has a cart and an old Percheron to pull it. The boy was about five or six, as I recall. He was doing something or other in the farmyard and Henry just did not see him. The wheel crushed his skull.

'Helen Madder would not forgive him. She turned quiet on him, staying inside, keeping him out of her room, locking herself away. Then, about six months after the tragedy, she put on her fanciest dress and went off to Bury to get herself a man. She found one soon enough, and people talked. Henry knew, but put up with it because he thought that the boy's death had been his fault. It wasn't, but nobody could persuade him otherwise. He thought that he deserved the punishment that she was doling out to him.

'Then she went off altogether and never came back. They say that she moved to Ipswich, but there were those who saw her in Newmarket – with the new man, who was some sort of market trader. Henry pretty much stopped talking to people after that. Stopped going to church. Stopped going to the pub. So that's Henry Madder – a good man ruined by one little bit of care-lessness. If he had moved his head just a few inches, just for a moment, he would have seen his boy and the accident wouldn't have taken place. But that's the same for everything, isn't it? If things were just a little bit different, then life would have worked out differently.

'Take that Mr Hitler. Just think what would have happened had his mother dropped him when she picked him up for his feed. And he had hit his head on the floor. Or had he been strangled by the cord when he was born. That happens to other babies; it could have happened to him. What a difference. We wouldn't be at war as we are right now. Wouldn't be in this pickle. Have you thought of that?'

La had not, and shook her head. 'Of course there could have been somebody else.'

'Other than Hitler? Somebody other than Hitler?'

'Yes. There could have been somebody else who would have had the same idea of whipping people up; who had the same madness within them. People are the products of their time, Mrs Agg.'

Mrs Agg glanced at her.

'What I mean, Mrs Agg, is that the times throw up their man. If there hadn't been a Nelson, there would have been another sailor like him. There would have been plenty of small, nasty people like Hitler, even if he had never existed.'

She let Mrs Agg think about this as she attached several pairs of socks to the line with large wooden clothes-pegs. She returned, though, to the subject of Madder Farm. 'Who was he, this boy who was helping him. The boy whose job I'm taking on?'

Mrs Agg, who had been holding a clothes-peg in her mouth while she attended to the socks, took the peg out of her mouth to answer. 'A nice boy. A really nice boy called Neil. The son of Mrs Howarth who used to work in the post office. He went off and volunteered. Who can blame him? That's what all young men want to do.'

La thought for a moment. All young men? What about Lennie? She tried to imagine Lennie in a uniform, but she could not. Mrs Agg glanced at her. She had guessed what her visitor was thinking.

'Lennie can't,' she said. 'Or, rather, I don't think he should.'

'But what if he wanted to? What if he wanted to join his friends?'

Mrs Agg give the socks a final, almost affectionate squeeze. 'Lennie can't be doing with friends, you know. He's a loner. He doesn't . . .'

She left the sentence unfinished, reaching for the last of her washing. Then, quietly, she said, 'Lennie doesn't trouble you, I hope.'

La looked up at the sky. After the incident in the garden, Lennie had not troubled her. In fact, she could barely remember when she had last seen him; it must have been months before, when she had driven past him on the road to Bury. He had been walking in the same direction, and she had slowed down, thinking that she might offer to drive him to wherever he was going, but he had pointedly looked over the hedge to his side, as if absorbed by something he saw in the field. She had driven on.

'Lennie doesn't trouble me, Mrs Agg. You needn't worry.'

Mrs Agg finished hanging up the rest of the washing and dried her hands on her apron. 'Good. You see, Mrs Stone . . . You see, Lennie is not all that easy. A lot of men aren't. But we get by.' She turned and smiled at La. 'Which is all that we can hope for in this life, don't you think? To get by?'

That was quite true, thought La, reductionist though the sentiment might be. In a way, all our human systems, our culture, music, literature, painting – all of that – was effectively an attempt to make life more bearable, to enable us to get by. She got by. She had got by, in this quiet corner of England, for two years now, and was happy enough where she was. She had stopped thinking of Richard every day, and she found it harder to bring up a mental image of the man who had been her husband. There was a face, certainly, but it was fading, as an old photograph will fade. What had his voice sounded like? He used to sing in the bath – she remembered that – but what were the words of the songs that he sang? She could not bring them to mind, and she no longer dreamed of him, or only did so very occasionally.

She was getting by quite well without him, as a widow. And the country was trying to get by in the face of a terrifying nightmare that was about to get much more vivid and more frightening.

'They're coming,' said the butcher in the village. 'They're coming over, Mrs Stone. God help us, so he must.'

'There's the RAF,' said La. 'They'll have to get past them.'

'Have you seen the boys they're using?' asked the butcher. There was a base nearby, at Stradishall, where the clay soil made good, hard runways for heavy bombers. 'Some of them not shaving yet, I think.'

'Boys have quick reactions,' said La. It was a glib remark, of the sort that came from inner conviction; but La felt despair. The strutting demagogue, with his insane shouting, had fixed his eyes on them, and he was coming.

Twelve

Poor Henry Madder, she thought; look at him. His hands had twisted, as if they had been placed in a vice and wrenched off true. And he could not bend his knees, which seemed to have locked at a forty-degree angle, giving him a curious, deliberate-looking gait, as if he were walking through a bed of treacle. But he did not complain and impatiently brushed off La's concern.

'Don't worry about me,' he said. 'As long as I can hook Tommy up to the plough, I'm all right. I'm not an old man yet.'

He was somewhere in his forties, La thought, but the crippling disease had aged him prematurely.

'I could do more here,' she said. 'It's much easier than I thought – looking after your chickens. There must be other things.'

He shook his head. 'I have to do something, and they've promised me a man, full-time. When they find one – whenever that will be.' He smiled. 'Heaven knows what I'll get. Somebody from Timbuktu maybe. Or a chap let out of prison on condition that he works on the land. Old Billy Stevens got somebody like that. A car thief from London, would you believe it? A Cockney spiv. He found him selling his eggs down at the pub.'

La's work was light. The chickens were kept on the edge of a field in two large coops. They were elongated, flimsily-built structures with tin roofs. Inside there were rows of nesting boxes and high, roughly-hewn perches on which the hens could take refuge at night from predators. There was also a fence that had been designed to protect the birds from the fox, but he could burrow his way under that, as the wire did not always reach far enough down. One of La's jobs was to pick up the feathers where the fox had made a kill; feathers that, with their occasional flecked blood stains, told the story of the sharp and one-sided little conflict. For La it was like attending a scene of the crime; the feathers on the ground, the hens clucking away in disapproval of what had happened – *move along please, madam, there is nothing to be seen here* – the place where the fox had pushed up the fence wire from its anchoring. There was always only one suspect.

La made her way up to Madder's Farm shortly after breakfast every day. She had to ride there; fuel was in short supply and she wanted to husband the small amount she could get. Cycling kept her fit, and it was pleasant enough, too, in the mild April weather; of course, it would be different in winter, with those dark mornings and the cold wind which in that part of England swept straight across the North Sea, from Siberia, it seemed. I shall be tougher then, she told herself, and if the war was over, then she would no longer have to work on Madder's Farm and could lie in bed on winter's mornings, as she had done last winter, watching her breath make white mist in the unheated air. Wars did not last forever; one hundred years at the most.

On arrival at the farm she reported to Henry if he was in the farmyard, or went directly about her duties if he was not. She collected the eggs first, making her way along the nesting boxes, taking out the eggs and placing them carefully in the large baskets that Henry provided. If a hen was still in the box, she would feel under her for eggs, amongst the soft, belly feathers, warm and downy, and the hens would occasionally peck at her, quite hard. She started to use gloves – an old pair of gardening gloves that she had found in the house, that Gerald must have used; the hens ineffectively pecked at the leather and La would blow in their faces to distract them.

She cleaned the floor below the perches and changed the straw in the nesting boxes. Then she filled a wheelbarrow with feed and distributed that amongst the brood. The acrid smell of the coops lingered; it was in her clothes. I smell like a chicken, she thought. I am a fox's dream.

Henry Madder said, 'You've taken to this like a duck to water.'

'Chicken,' she said.

He smiled. 'They said you didn't want any pay. Is that correct?'

'I have enough to live on,' La said. 'I have more than enough. If they don't pay me, then the money can go to other land army workers.'

He looked at her intently. 'You're the type who'll win this war for us,' he said.

'There are people working far harder than I am,' said La. 'Miners, for instance.'

Henry thought about this. 'That's something I could never do. Go underground. Crawl around in the darkness. At least we get fresh air in our work. It may be cold and dirty sometimes, but there's fresh air.'

He looked up at the sky, and La followed his gaze. It was broad, limitless, unclouded now; the wide sky of East Anglia.

She took her leave and began the cycle back. She reached home at about half past eleven every morning, her labours done. Then she read, and worked in the garden. She had started to sew, thinking it might be useful; she could make things for people when clothing became scarce. Everything would become scarce, she thought; soap, clothing, shoes. Hitler wanted to starve them into submission, and they would have to grub around, turning to every little bit of earth to coax food from it. She looked at her lawn. She would dig it up and plant potatoes. It could yield sacks of potatoes that would see her through the winter, if supplies of everything dried up.

Henry Madder gave her eggs, which she turned into omelettes. There were chives in the garden, and these were chopped up to add flavour. She ate the omelettes at her kitchen table, a glass of cider beside her plate. She would have liked to talk to somebody, but the house was empty.

Occasionally, after one of her lonely suppers, La would retrieve the flute that she kept in a drawer in her bureau. She had rarely played the instrument since leaving Cambridge, and her technique had suffered. But she could still manage most of the pieces in a large book of flute music she had found in a second-hand bookshop near the British Museum: Byrd, Morley, Tallis. At Cambridge she had played a madrigal called 'In Nets of Golden Wires'. She thought it was by Morley, and she was sure it was in her book, but when she paged through the arrangements she could not find it. The title haunted her. What did it mean? Was it about love, or belonging, or about capturing a dream?

Music was her refuge. There was madness abroad, an insanity

of killing and cruelty that defied understanding – unless one took the view that this violence had always been there and had merely been masked by a veneer of civilisation. La thought that music disproved this. Reason, beauty, harmony: these were ultimately more real and powerful than any of the demons unleashed by dictators. But she feared that she was losing touch with these values – that her life in the country was simply too limited. She feared that she would forget if she did not go back.

One evening, when she had finished her dinner and had sat reading for half an hour at the kitchen table, she reached a decision. She would return to London where the house in Maida Vale could be reclaimed from its tenant. She would take up with her old friends and bring an end to this unnatural life of seclusion. She wanted company; particularly the company of people of her own age, of her own outlook. She wanted to talk to somebody about books, about music, about the things that nobody seemed to talk about here. There were people in Bury, of course, with whom she had interests in common, but that was Bury, and there was no petrol to go there for purely social purposes. Cambridge would have been even better, but was further away, and she could not go back there; people who did that ended up like Dr Price.

She telephoned Valerie. 'I want to come back to London,' she said. 'I've made up my mind.'

There was silence at the other end of the line. Then, 'Are you mad?'

'I don't know what you mean. Why is it mad to want to come back to London?'

Valerie laughed. 'But, listen La: anybody with any sense is

trying to get *out* of London. Have you heard of the Luftwaffe down there in Suffolk?'

La said nothing.

'The point is,' Valerie continued, 'the point is that this is a very different city from the one you left.'

La understood that places changed. 'I know that. I don't expect it to be the same. I've changed.'

Valerie laughed dismissively. 'I don't think you're grasping what I want to say. People are frightened, La. Anybody who is in a position to leave is thinking about it. They deny it, of course, but then everybody's trying to look brave. We have to, because if we started to show what we really felt the whole place would come to a grinding halt. In fact, we're frightened. London is not the place to be.'

It was hard to argue against such a warning, and La did not. Their conversation continued briefly and without much under-standing; it seemed to La that they now lived in different worlds. Then the allotted three minutes was up; La said goodbye and rang off.

La lived too far from the base at Stradishall to hear the planes taking off and landing, but now, at frequent intervals, she heard the drone of engines as a flight of bombers crossed the sky. Like everyone else, she had studied the outlines printed in the news-papers so that she could distinguish plane from plane, but it was hard to tell when they were little more than black dots against the white of the clouds. Spitfires, of course, were easily recog-nised, and over that summer and into the autumn she looked out for them. The battle had begun – the battle that would deter-mine the course of the war – everyone knew that. And the

Spitfire, with its stubby wings and its long nose, would, along with the Hurricane, determine the fate of the country – and the world. They had to win this part of it; if Britain fell, then Europe was lost to a devouring evil, and that evil would not stop at Europe.

One afternoon she saw a Spitfire coming in from the coast. The main battle was being fought further to the south, but planes would sometimes chase raiders up over the North Sea until they reached the limit of their range and had to make for home. This one was flying low and was trailing smoke, limping across the sky to refuge at Stradishall. She watched it getting lower and lower and she thought of the pilot within. Sometimes nothing but air separates those who are in deadly peril from those who are safe. He would be twenty; perhaps even younger; a young man struggling to keep his wounded aircraft airborne, gasping for breath against the fumes from his burning plane. And then the plane was gone, vanished behind distant trees, and she did not know what had happened. Mrs Agg said that the pilot had made it back to the airfield, but Mrs Agg was optimistic about these things; she did not really know. She wanted him to be safe, and so she said that he was.

An air force officer called at the house one day. He had been given La's name by a cousin of hers who was working in Whitehall and who met officers in the course of her work. He drove up to the house one Saturday afternoon, parking his small green open-topped car in the driveway.

'I'm very sorry turning up out of the blue,' he said when La opened the door to him. 'I'm Tim Honey. I'm a friend of Lilly's. She said that I should call on you if I was in the area.'

La looked at the man standing on her doorstep. He was about

her age, or perhaps a few years older, in his mid-thirties, and slightly plump. His uniform, she noticed, was pulled tight across the front. Rations, she thought; and then silently upbraided herself: if one was to die, as these men expected to, then they should at least be given good breakfasts.

She invited him in. 'I don't have any coffee,' she said. 'But I have some tea.'

Tim smiled, and fished in one of the pockets of his jacket. 'I anticipated that,' he said, drawing out a small packet. 'This is Jamaican, believe it or not. I don't know how we got it at the base, but it suddenly appeared. I think that our Canadian friends shipped it across. He laughed. 'It's amazing what you find in the back of a bomber once you begin to unpack it.'

She took the packet and led the way into the kitchen. 'Lilly,' she said.

'Yes, dear Lilly. She says she hasn't seen you for ages.'

'No. I moved down here a few years ago, before the war started.' She wondered if he would think that she had fled from London. She did not want him to think that.

He nodded. He was looking about the kitchen, appraisingly.

'I've got everything I need in this house,' said La. 'It's really quite comfortable.'

'Yes. It looks it.' He turned towards the window. 'They look after us pretty well at the base. We can't really complain. We have a very good mess – all the papers and magazines and your jolly good Suffolk beers. Everything we need, really.'

There was a silence. Except company, thought La. Except women. Home cooking. Love.

'I'm married,' Tim went on. 'Four years ago. And I never thought that this would blow up and I'd find myself at one end of the country and Joyce at the other end. She's in Cardiff, staying with an aunt for the duration. It's safer there, I think, than where we lived in Kent. In Maidstone. That's pretty much in the thick of things at the moment.'

'You must miss her.'

'Yes, I do. Awfully. But think of all those chaps who have been sent overseas. Or the chaps out East. What chance have they got of seeing their wives? At least I can go down for the occasional weekend.'

The smell of coffee began to pervade. La took a deep breath. It reminded her of Cambridge, for some reason. Dr Price; that was it. Dr Price had served coffee at her very first supervision, when she had been nervous. 'Coffee will clear your head,' she had said. 'It always works.' And they had drunk a small cup of strong coffee and then Dr Price had sat there with a rather pained expression on her face as La had read the first essay she had written.

'We can drink our coffee in here,' said La. 'There's a drawing room of sorts, but it's more comfortable in here.'

'I'm happy,' said Tim, laying his cap down on the table. 'I should have changed into civvies, but sometimes, when you're visiting people, they like to see the uniform.'

They talked. Tim told her about what he had done before the war and what he did now, approximately. 'I shouldn't say exactly,' he said. 'Not that I imagine you're a German spy, but you know the rules. Suffice it to say that I sit behind a desk all day and talk on the telephone, telling other people what we want. I'm in charge of supplies for the whole base. Not that I should probably tell you that. Do you know anywhere where I could get some supplies of aviation fuel?'

La laughed. 'Or Jamaican coffee?'

'We're all right for that. Fuel is the big thing. I live in fear of what might happen if they really get going on despatching our tankers to the bottom of the ocean with their U-boats. What then? You can't fight a battle for control of the skies if your planes can't take off.'

They talked about what La was doing. She told him about the chickens, and her battle against the fox.

'Gerry's a fox,' said Tim. 'Trying to get in under the chicken wire. And Goering's the biggest fox of all.'

Her own war, as she looked upon it, was so small by comparison with his: a few eggs added to the national supply, that was all. She told him about Henry Madder and of his determination to continue farming, in spite of his arthritis.

'They've been promising him somebody,' she said. 'But he must be at the bottom of the list. A smallish farm, tucked away out of sight. The bigger places will be getting whoever becomes available.'

Tim frowned. 'I know how he must feel. I have to ask for aircraft. I have to ask for all sorts of things and often they just ignore your requests. They tell you that you'll get things shortly, but it's never like that.' He paused. 'He'd be paid?'

'I assume so,' said La. 'I'm not, but I said that I didn't need it. Henry paid the boy who helped him. And he's got a cottage on the farm that's empty. The boy stayed there.'

Tim looked up at the ceiling. 'I might know somebody.'

'To work?'

He nodded. 'Yes. We've got a Polish chap. Feliks Dabrowski. We call him Dab for short. Like most of those people he's had a pretty frustrating war. He got out to Romania and then to

France. They set up something called the Groupe de Chasse Polonaise there and gave them worse than useless planes. The Gerries shot them out of the sky. Dab was badly hurt – lost the use of an eye, in fact, although it looks almost normal to me. But he's blind as a bat on that side.'

La sighed. 'Poor man. Mind you, he's alive. Which is something these days.'

'Indeed it is. You know how many we've lost in just one of our squadrons . . .' He stopped himself. 'Sorry, I shouldn't talk about that.'

'I can imagine.'

'It's hard . . .'

She was not sure what to say. 'Yes. Your men are so brave.'

Tim shook his head. 'No, they aren't. Well, maybe some are, but most of us are just very ordinary, and scared stiff half the time. When I was on active flying duty, before I had trouble with my back, I remember shaking when I got out of the cockpit at the end of a sortie. I knew that my number was up – that I had defied the odds and that they would catch up with me sooner or later. I knew that. And I was not at all brave about it. Nightmares. Sweating. Stomach turning to water. I had all of that.'

He reached for his coffee cup and drained it. 'But this chap, Dab, I was talking about. He pitched up when the Poles started to get out of France. One of our medical officers looked after him – tried to do something about his eye, but couldn't. So there was no chance of any more flying for him. And he had nowhere to go, so we kept him on the base, gave him maintenance duties and so on. But you can't let a chap with one eye tinker with the planes – he might get it wrong. Too risky. So we need to find something for him.'

La listened. She had heard the stories of other displaced persons; there were so many of them. 'You think that he might work for Henry Madder?'

'Well, it would suit both of them, don't you think? Dab hasn't got a bean and he would get a bit of money, and presumably his rations. And a roof over his head.'

La shrugged. 'I could ask Henry.'

Tim stood up and reached for his cap. 'Let me do that,' he said. 'Tell me how to get there and I'll go and have a word with him.'

He started to leave, but stopped when he saw La's flute on the kitchen dresser. 'You play?'

'A bit. I played in a quartet when I was in Cambridge. And you?'

'As a matter of fact,' said Tim. 'I was a very indifferent trumpet player in my day.'

La smiled. 'We could hardly play together. The flute, I'm afraid, is a rather quiet instrument.'

'We have chaps at the base who would love to play in a band,' said Tim. 'One of them came to see me the other day and asked whether I could get hold of instruments. I ask you! I've got my hands full enough as it is getting spares and tyres and what not. And they asked me for a couple of clarinets.'

La said nothing. It had occurred to her that she might be able to do something. The idea came suddenly, as perfectly formed ideas sometimes do. She would start an orchestra. She would get instruments for the men at the base who wanted them. She would find people in Bury who would join in. People needed something to keep their spirits up.

'What if I got hold of some instruments?' she asked Tim.

'Would your men be able to come and play music with some locals? People from Bury, people from round here – if I found any who could play.'

Tim hesitated. 'It would depend. Most of them can't get away very much. And transport is always a problem.'

'Once every few weeks,' said La. 'Or even once a month.'

'Once a month would be more likely.'

'So you don't object?'

Tim scratched the back of his neck. 'I'll ask the C.O.'

'Call it morale boosting,' said La. 'That works, doesn't it?'

Again he hesitated before replying. 'Yes. It does. And this seems like a good idea. La's Orchestra. How about that?'

'And you'll be in the trumpet section?' asked La.

'I thought you were never going to ask,' Tim said. 'Yes. You can sign me up.'

Thirteen

It was raining when La cycled over to the farm the next morning. She had not expected the rain and was unprepared for it; by the time she cycled into the farmyard, she was soaked, her hair across her forehead in thin, wet ropes, her blouse clinging uncomfortably to her skin.

Henry Madder, standing in the yard in his heavy green waterproof jacket, seemed amused. 'You look a sight. Like a mouse washed down the drainpipe.'

La leaned her bicycle against the side of the house. 'Thank you,' she said. 'It's nice to start the day with a compliment.'

'No compliments on a farm.'

'Yes. So I'm discovering.'

He smiled. 'Come inside and dry off. I'll get you a towel, and you can have a hot bath if you like. I'll stoke up the fire.'

She went with him into the kitchen. A kettle stood on the range, steam emerging from the spout in wisps. While he fetched her a towel, La warmed her hands against the cooking range; the rain had been warm, and there had been no wind with it;

so she did not feel too cold. It was the wind that could chill one to the bone; the east wind that seemed effortlessly to find its way past such saliences as the landscape threw up. 'Don't bother,' she shouted after Henry. 'I'm sure I'll dry off quickly enough.'

But he was back in the kitchen bearing a voluminous white towel. He handed it to her. 'I had a visitor yesterday,' he said. 'Your friend, Squadron-Leader Honey.'

'I only met him yesterday,' said La. 'So I can hardly call him a friend just yet.'

'He said he knew your cousin,' Henry went on. 'Not that it matters. The point is: he's got somebody to help us. He's coming tomorrow.'

La smiled. 'The man they call Dab?'

'Feliks something or other,' said Henry. 'Dab comes into it. A Polish airman. He told me that these Poles are real characters. Our boys are always a bit afraid that they'll do something silly.'

'I'm sure that he'll do nothing silly on the farm,' said La. 'Tractors and Spitfires are rather different, don't you think?'

Henry Madder sat down at the other side of the table. He watched La drying herself on the towel; hair first, forearms, then her face. She was conscious of his gaze and felt slightly uncomfortable under it; but there was nothing sexual in his watching her, she thought. She could not conceive of Henry in that light, but he must have had a love life, once, before he was abandoned.

'Will you be going?' Henry suddenly asked.

La did not understand. 'Going where?'

'Leaving the farm? Stopping work.'

La laid aside the towel. 'Why would I want to stop work? Because of this Pole?'

'Yes. If he's here, then he can do the chickens.'

La shook her head. 'I want to carry on with that. If it's all right with you. It's my war work, you see . . .'

It was clear that Henry was relieved. 'Yes. Yes. There are plenty of other things for him to do,' he said. 'And the hens are used to you, aren't they?'

La greeted this with laughter. 'Can they tell us one from another, do you think?'

'Hens know,' said Henry. 'Hens feel more comfortable with a woman. They were upset when Helen . . .' He broke off. La looked up, and saw him turn his face away. It was the first time that she had heard him mention his wife.

'When she left you?'

'Yes. When she left, the hens were unsettled. I think they went off their lay. They missed her.'

La reached for the towel again. A trickle of moisture ran down the back of her neck.

She spoke quietly. 'You mustn't blame yourself, you know. Accidents happen, and then people look around for somebody to blame. It's human nature, I suppose, but it's not very helpful.'

He was watching her intently, as if she had in her possession information of great importance – the key to some conundrum that had been bothering him. 'Do you think so?'

'Of course I do. You shouldn't let yourself be tormented by something like that.'

He thought about this for a moment. She saw that he was rubbing at the edge of his jacket with his misshapen hand, kneading the waxed material.

'You can't undo what's done,' he said after a while. 'Nobody can.'

'No.'

He nodded. 'I still feel bad. How could I not feel bad?'

'By understanding that it was not your fault.'

He turned away again. 'She didn't think that. She thought it was my fault.'

'Perhaps she felt guilty herself. And if she did, then one of the ways in which she might deal with that would be to blame you. If we blame other people, it makes our own guilt much easier to live with.'

He stood up from the table. 'Maybe,' he said. 'Maybe not. But I have to go out and look at a fence. And the hens will be waiting for you.'

La followed his example and rose from the table. 'You will think about what I've just said? You will think about it?'

'Maybe. Not now. Maybe later.'

She decided to change the subject. 'Will he live in the cottage?'

'Yes. I'm getting it ready today.'

La could not imagine Henry doing housework. Surely it would be difficult for him to hold a broom, in those hands of his; it would certainly be painful.

'I'll do that,' she offered. 'After I've done the chickens.'

'You don't have to.'

'I know. But we want our Polish airman to be comfortable, don't we?'

He gave her the key to the cottage. The guttering had leaked immediately above the front door, with the result that the wood was stained and swollen. The key turned easily enough in the lock, but then La was obliged to push at the door with all her strength before it opened.

It was dark inside. The curtains in the living room – the room one entered directly from the front door – had been drawn closed and there was no light from any source other than the door. She moved across the room and drew the curtains back. A musty odour rose from the cloth, and there was also a smell emanating from the back of the house, from the kitchen.

The cottage was very small: a sitting room, furnished with two easy chairs over which stained, threadbare rugs had been thrown; the kitchen, where there was a small dining table; and a tiny single bedroom. There was no bath, just a tin tub that had been stacked against the wall of the bedroom. A large china ewer, chipped around the rim, stood beside the tub.

She looked about her for a switch to turn on a light; even after she had tugged at the curtains, there was little natural sunlight in any of the rooms. But there were no switches anywhere, and then she noticed the oil-lamp on the kitchen table, and the saucer in which a half-used candle still stood, a pool of hardened melted wax at its base.

For the rest of that morning she swept, scrubbed and polished. She cleaned out the tub, which had rings of recalcitrant scum about its sides; she swept the ashes out of the fireplace in the sitting room and removed the black lumps which had dislodged from the chimney and fallen onto the lino; she washed from the floor the black stains the soot had created. She lifted the coir mattress in the bedroom and shook it vigorously; fine dust flew up in small clouds, making her cough; cobwebs, dislodged from exposed beams fell across her shoulders like delicate lace mantles.

Henry had followed her in with sheets and blankets, which she now put on the bed. A patchwork counterpane, which had been draped over a chair, fitted the bed exactly. With that in place, and with the floor swept, the bedroom looked inhabitable, and, from there, slowly the rest of the cottage was transformed.

Henry returned later, bringing La a mug of tea. He had not made tea for her before and he had not asked her whether she took sugar or not – she did not. The tea he presented her with was sweet and sickly, but La was thankful for it. She had run out of tea that week, and she was happy to drink what Henry provided.

'You've made it very nice for him, La,' said Henry, gazing about him.

'He's far from home,' said La. 'And he'll be fed up with living in the barracks and places like that. We need to make it look homely.'

Henry was silent. 'It could happen to us, I suppose. We could be uprooted. Chucked out of our homes – if they invade.'

'Yes,' said La.

'I wish I could get out there and take a pot shot at them,' said Henry. 'I feel useless.'

'You couldn't,' said La. 'You know that. And you're doing more than enough, as it is. Our boys have to eat.'

'Oh, I know,' said Henry. 'But it's not the same.'

La put down her duster. 'What do you think he'll be like, this Pole?'

'Oh, he'll be all right,' said Henry. 'They're nice people. So folks say.'

'I'll cook something for him tomorrow. I'll bring it over. He'll get used to looking after himself, no doubt, but for the first day . . .'

'You'll spoil him.'

'Maybe,' said La. 'But don't you think that he'll deserve it?'

She did not sleep well that night. Somewhere in the small hours she was woken by the sound of aircraft overhead. She lay in bed listening as the engine noise slowly became louder, thinking: this is what people hear when bombers come. And it could be that this plane was a German plane, laden with bombs that it could drop at any moment; bomber crews did that – if they could not find their target, they would drop the bombs anywhere, in the hope of hitting something – a house, a factory, a woman lying alone in her bed looking up into the night. But the engine drone began to fade as the plane headed off.

She imagined the men in the plane, sitting there in their darkened cabins, going about their business of death and destruction. They would have no qualms, of course, because they would know the justice of their cause – whichever side they were on. She tried to picture German flyers, but the image eluded her. What sort of faces would they have? The same as ours, of course. And their feelings? Fear, perhaps, of exactly the same sort as our men experienced.

But of course they were not like us. These men were ruthless; they were the men who flew the wailing Stukas that strafed the columns of refugees – they were not men like Tim Honey; not at all. She had read an account of a British airman who witnessed German pilots shooting men who were floating down by parachute: they shot them in cold blood, riddling their bodies with the very ammunition they used to down aircraft; nobody could stand a chance against that. They shot prisoners, too, and civilians in reprisal for attacks on occupying forces. No, she could bring herself to hate them, these strutting scions of the Master Race; she could so easily bring herself to hate them. Hate was easy because it was simply so human.

She lay in bed thinking of this – of what the war was doing to people. By six o'clock, she realised that she had not slept since half past two, and now it would be too late. If she went back to sleep now – and she was feeling drowsy enough for that – then she might sleep in late, and she could not keep the chickens waiting. Anyway, this was the day on which the Pole arrived.

She felt strangely responsible for him. Surely she should feel indifferent towards him – there were so many displaced persons, people washed up by the war, people from somewhere else – and yet already she felt that looking after him was something that she had to do. But why? Because he was in need and he was about to cross her path. That, perhaps, was the basis of our responsibility to one another; the simple fact that we collided with one another. She would be kind to him; even in normal times it was hard enough trying to make a go of living in England when one did not belong; how much more difficult must it be in times of fear and suspicion, in times of shortage. Poles were Catholic, of course, and there was a Catholic priest in Bury, a shy Irishman who blushed when you talked to him, something of a figure of fun in the town, or so she had heard. She had bumped into him in the bookshop there once and he had sufficiently overcome his shyness to converse for half an hour or so about a book that La had taken from the shelves. She would speak to the priest and ask him to take him under his wing.

After breakfast she set out for the farm. Yesterday's clouds had been blown away by a change in the wind, and the morning sky was high and open. This was good weather for bombers in search of targets, but it would also be good news for the RAF, who liked a sun out of which to swoop. Things were getting worse now; the battle was intense. Every day, almost without let-up, flights of marauders came in, wave upon wave of them, hammering hard at England. Frighten them, said Hitler; terrify them into submission. But the onslaught had the opposite effect, and strengthened resolve. Every day the RAF committed virtually all its men and machines to the air in desperate sorties, one after the other, mercilessly. She had heard of pilots going to sleep at the controls of their aircraft, utterly exhausted, pushed beyond any normal human limits; she had heard of them drinking before they went up, trying to dull the fear, to obliterate their knowledge of the odds.

And here, in spite of all that was happening only a short way away, was a summer morning, with ripening ears of wheat, of barley, swaying in the wind, with a man walking a dog alongside a hedgerow, with a knot of sheep around a tin hopper, waiting for salt-cake. Manna, thought La; animals believe in manna because for them it is quite real: food appears. And if we believed in the possibility of manna, then what might we want now? For the heavens to open and a cornucopia of arms to be disgorged upon the land? Tanks, gleaming planes, shiny rifles, fountains of petrol and oil.

Before the war, she had kept a lingering belief in God, not much more than a few scraps from the religious education she had received at school: the sermon on the mount, the walking on water, the wedding feast at Cana. At a wedding or a christening she would bow her head and go through the motions, along with everybody else, but the words, beautiful though they might be, were empty oncs, for her at least, no more than shibboleths uttered because it was expected of one. Then the idea of God had become weaker and weaker until it had faded altogether, to become a recollection of somebody she used to know vaguely, but whose memory had become attenuated, like that of an old uncle met once in childhood. The war had convinced her that he simply was not there. If he were, then how could he not intervene? It would be so simple for God to dispose of Hitler. He would only have to raise a finger, just a finger, and flick him out of the way; and do the same for Goering and his air force too. How satisfying it would be for a divine hand to knock the bombers out of the air. Imagine their surprise! But there was no divine hand, she told herself; we are in this quite alone. It was perfectly possible for might to triumph, because that was what human history had shown all along: might prevailed.

Lost in her thoughts, she did not see the car until it was almost upon her. She had plenty of time to stop, though, to dismount and pull her bicycle over to the side; the road was too narrow there for both of them and cycles gave way to motor vehicles. Again it was a question of might.

The driver wound down his window and inched the car forward until it was level with her.

'Early to work, I see.'

She smiled. It was Tim Honey, driving a different car. This was an official one, a dark blue Austin with a military number plate.

'I didn't recognise you. Your nice little sports car . . .'

He tapped his hand on the wheel. 'This goes with the job. I use my own for social purposes – when I can lay my hands on any petrol for it. And when I'm fortunate enough for social purposes to turn up.'

Tim jerked his head in the direction of the farm. 'I've just dropped Dab – Feliks, rather, up there. I saw the billet you'd prepared for him. Madder said it was all your work. Well done.'

'It was a bit dark and dingy,' said La. 'I wanted him to be moderately comfortable.'

'Moderately comfortable? He can't believe his luck! He said he couldn't remember when he last had a room to himself.'

Tim glanced at his watch. 'I mustn't linger, I'm afraid. We're very busy right now, and I'm due back on duty in half an hour. By the way . . .'

La knew what he was going to ask. 'My orchestra?'

'Yes. I spoke to those chaps I mentioned, and to a couple of others. They're very keen.'

'So you might be able to fix something up?'

'Yes. And Dab plays the flute too, you know. He hasn't got one, but when I told him about our conversation he let slip that he used to play. He's an educated man, you know. A lot of those Poles are. You think you know them, and then you discover something extraordinary about them – that they had a big factory somewhere, or were trained as doctors, or were becoming priests when this business all started. All that sort of thing.' He sighed. 'It makes it even tougher for them, I think. To lose your country and your family and everything – position, respect and all the rest . . . Well, that can't be easy.'

'We'll try to look after him.'

Tim smiled and stretched a hand out of the window of the car. She shook it.

La leaned her bicycle against the wall and bent down to remove the cycle clips that she placed about her trouser legs. She wore trousers for her work on the farm; not the most glamorous of outfits, she said, but very practical: strong gaberdine trousers of worsted that she had brought with her from London. Straight-. ening up, she saw a light in Henry Madder's kitchen, a dark room that received little sun. Even so, Henry was not one to waste electricity, or anything for that matter, and La had imagined him at night, with no lights on, fumbling about in the dark. The light, then, was in honour of Feliks.

She approached the back door and knocked.

'We're in here,' Henry called out. 'Come right in, La.'

When La entered the room, she saw Henry standing near the range, holding the kettle, which he was about to put on the plate. At the table, half turned round to face her, sat a man wearing a leather jacket of the sort favoured by pilots; this one, though, was worn, the leather cracked about the shoulders and at the cuffs. La's first thought was that it was too warm to be wearing that, but then she saw that he had a thin, collarless shirt under-neath. And below that, dark trousers, of what looked to her like thin linen. When she entered, he sprang to his feet and stood facing her.

'Dabrowski,' he said, inclining his head. 'Feliks Dabrowski.'

La moved forward. He had extended his hand towards her.

'This is my other assistant,' said Henry. 'La Stone. The saviour of the hens.'

'I suspect that the hens would get by quite well without me,' said La.

Henry shook his head. He was very literal. 'No, they wouldn't.'

La glanced at Feliks. He looked younger than she had imagined; not as boyish as some of those pilots, but certainly younger than the thirty-four that Tim Honey had mentioned. Twenty-eight, perhaps. And he was definitely Slav; she could tell from the smoothness of the cheeks and the high cheekbones; it was a quite different look, an almost feminine beauty. His eyes: she wondered which one was the one that had been ruined. Would she be able to tell, or would she have to ask? It was potentially disconcerting, as it always was when one did not know which eye to look at. One might be gazing into the wrong eye, talking to that eye, so to speak, while all the time the other eye was watching one.

'The left eye,' said Henry, pushing the kettle onto the plate with his twisted hand. 'Feliks was telling me. He lost the sight in his left eye in action.'

La dropped her gaze guiltily. 'I'm sorry to hear that.'

Feliks sat down now. 'Thank you. I have become used to it. You can get by with one of most things. There are men at the base with one leg or one arm. They get by too.'

His accent was certainly foreign, yet it was still clear enough and had a soft lilt to it, akin, La thought, to the way in which a Swede would speak English.

'La will show you the hen houses,' said Henry. 'Just so that you know everything that's going on. But she does all the work down there.'

Feliks looked at La and smiled. 'That will be good.'

There was a silence. La waited for something more to be said, but neither man spoke. She looked at the kettle. Henry's range was always slow; it would take ten minutes for the water to boil. She would have liked to stay, but had no idea what she would say. Henry would not waste his words, and Feliks seemed shy. It would be strange for him, this farm, with this rather unusual farmer. And he would be wondering what her own role was, apart from tending the hens.

'I'll get on with things,' she said.

Henry Madder nodded and Feliks rose to his feet again as La turned to the door. He rose automatically, as one in whom a chivalrous response had been inculcated. She thought, *This is not a man who will be used to working on a farm.* She wondered what he had been before the war. That was the extraordinary thing about what the war achieved: it transformed lives, made heroes out of the mildest of people, out of the most timid, showed the bravery that must always have been there but merely lacked the occasion to manifest itself. It revealed other things too: greed and selfishness disclosed their hand as people faced the prospect of hardship or hunger. She wondered whether she herself had changed, and decided that she was probably unexcitedly in the middle, where she had always felt she belonged. Would she cheat to get petrol? No. Would she take risks, imperil her life, if the situation required it? Equally no.

She made her way to the hen houses, where she worked for the next two hours. The fox had been active the previous night, having dug up a small section of chicken wire at the end of the run. There were feathers on the ground below one of the laying boxes, a broken egg and, at the end of one of the hen houses, obscured by shadows, the limp body of a hen, half of a wing torn off. The scattered feathers were clearly from a different hen, and from this La deduced that the fox had killed more than he needed and had been unable to carry away his second victim.

When she had finished the repairs and had fed the chickens, she picked up the dead hen and carried it back to the house. Seeing her approach, Henry came out and examined the dead fowl.

'The devil!' he said. 'He kills out of spite. What animal does that, La?'

'Cats,' said La. And added, 'Men.'

Henry took the hen from her and shook his head. 'A fine layer, no doubt. What a waste!' He handed it back to her. 'See if he wants it. Him.' He jerked his head in the direction of the cottage. 'He looks as if he could do with a bit of feeding up. A nice chicken casserole will go down well there, I suspect.'

'You take it.'

Henry shook his head. 'No you. I need to sit down. Take it to him. He's getting himself sorted out and will be starting work after lunch. Take it.'

She left him and walked over towards the cottage. Feliks must have seen her from the window, as he appeared at the door as she approached it.

'This is for you. A fox killed it.'

He frowned. 'They are a nuisance.'

'Round here they are.'

He reached for the chicken. 'Thank you.' He looked at it, holding it up and then putting it down on a shelf to the side of the door. 'What do you say? Waste not . . .'

'Want not.'

'Yes. That's it.'

For a few moments he examined the chicken. It seemed to La that he was contemplating it with regret, and that surprised her. Then he looked up, and rubbed his hands on his trousers; the hen had begun to bleed, and there was blood on his hands. He should wipe it off, she thought, because it would coagulate and then smell if left where it was.

She turned to go.

'You are kind. People have been so kind. Everyone. The English.'

She stopped. It had not occurred to her that the English would be judged by others. 'Really?'

'Yes. Very kind.'

'I thought that maybe you met with . . . well, the opposite. Suspicion. Selfishness. What are you doing here? That sort of thing.'

He shook his head. 'There might be a little of that. But not usually. Usually it's kindness. The English are a kind people.' He paused. 'Maybe they don't know it.'

La waited for him to say something else, but that was the end of his observations on the English national character.

'Oh well. Maybe.' She turned away again and left him. He took the chicken in and closed the door.

She walked back to her bicycle, fastened the cycle clips around her ankles, and set off on the ride home. The day had become warmer, the sun floating up the sky, painting the top of Henry Madder's wheat crop with streaks of gold. She cycled slowly, thinking. Something had happened, something within her. It was an unsettling feeling, something she was not prepared for and had not imagined she would feel again. A mile or two down the lane, she stopped and dismounted from her bicycle. It was at a point where a small clump of willow trees grew behind the unruly hedgerow bordering the road. There was a gap here, just enough to let her through – a gap that had been made by the boys from the nearby village, perhaps, or by lovers seeking a quiet place away from the eyes of others. She crawled through, and then flopped down on a bank of grass next to the willows. She looked up. The sky was quite cloudless, a singing, echoing emptiness.

This good place, this kind country, so gentle, so threatened. She lay back and closed her eyes. The strange, unsettling feeling was still with her; curiously, it made her aware of just how much she loved the piece of earth upon which she lay, that particular grass, that particular tiny patch of Suffolk.

Fourteen

Over the weeks that followed, La saw very little of Feliks. There was no sign of him when she arrived for work, nor when she left.

'How's he settling in?' she asked Henry Madder when he came down to the hen houses to inspect the place where La had fixed the fence.

'Just fine. He's a hard worker. Your Squadron-Leader friend was right.'

'He said that he was a good worker?'

Henry kicked at the fence repair to test its strength.

'Nice job, La. No, he just said that he was a good man. Amounts to the same thing I suppose.' Henry kicked at the fence again. The repair held. 'Damn fox. Damn war. The hunt can't feed enough dogs. All that meat they need. So old fox gets away with murder.'

La sighed. 'Poor hens. They have no idea there's a war on.'

'Lucky them.'

La brought the conversation back to Feliks. 'Where is he? I haven't seen him.'

Henry pointed towards the far end of the farm. 'Down there. Pott's field. He's digging drainage. I've been meaning to do that for years, and now we can get it done. Pott's has always been too marshy. If we drain it properly we can get a winter crop maybe this year.'

She saw him, though, a few days later, when she was just about to finish work. Henry had asked him to take a break from the drainage and cut grass for fodder; he was using a scythe, and had taken his shirt off for the heat. La watched him for a few moments, and then, fastening the hen-run door, she made her way up to Henry's kitchen.

Henry was sitting at the table with an open account book before him. He looked up when La entered.

'If I had to pay you and Feliks proper wages,' he said, 'I'd be bankrupt.'

'You don't expect me to believe that, Henry,' said La.

'Believe it or not, it's true.'

'I think that you're one of these farmers who keeps a lot of money under his bed, or in a cupboard somewhere.' She had read about just such a case; the farmer had died and his daughter had discovered six thousand pounds in a bag under the stairs.

Henry moved in his seat. Just slightly. 'What makes you say that?' There was an edge to his voice.

'Oh, just a suspicion.' La moved to the sink, a large Belfast. 'Anyway, I'd like to take him some water,' she said. 'It must be hot work, out there in the sun.'

'There's lemonade in the cupboard,' said Henry. 'Take a look. Go on. He deserves it.'

She found the large bottle and poured a glass.

'And you?' said Henry. 'You can have some if you like.'

'I don't really deserve it,' said La. 'He's the one who's been working.'

She went out with the glass of lemonade on a small tray and made her way down to the field. Feliks saw her coming before she arrived, and he stopped working, leaning on his scythe, waiting for her. She gave him the lemonade and he took it and drank it in one draught. He smiled at her, as if in triumph at the short work he had made of the drink, handing her back the empty glass.

The feeling that she had experienced came back. She felt her heart thumping. Ridiculous, she thought. Ridiculous. She looked down at the ground, at the blade of the scythe, at the shoes he was wearing, boots that had badly-scuffed toes.

She felt the glass, cool to the touch, moist with condensation. 'Would you like to come and have a meal at my house? Tonight?'

She surprised herself. This had not been planned.

He moved his hands on the handle of the scythe. 'Yes, I would like that.'

'Good.'

'You must show me how to get there. Henry says there is a bicycle . . .'

La explained and he listened. She gave him the directions and left him. Up at the house, Henry wordlessly took the glass from her and returned to the scrutiny of his account book. But then, a few moments later, he looked up and said, 'Don't go and get any silly ideas about that Pole.'

La caught her breath. 'What I do or don't do is none of your business, Henry. Thank you.'

He assumed a pained expression. 'Sorry! I was only thinking of you. Men could take advantage of you, you see.'

La's answer was cold. 'Thank you for worrying about me.'

I am not in love, she said to herself. I am finished with love.

When she returned to the house that morning, the postman had delivered a letter from Tim, written on RAF stationery. 'I have spoken to the C.O. about your orchestra,' he wrote. 'He was a bit sceptical at first, but he's like that about every idea that anybody comes up with. He pointed out that there were so many comings and goings that it would be difficult to have any continuity. Then he said that if we had anything, we should have a station band. And that idea, he said, had already been rejected: nobody to organise it.

'So I persisted, because that's the way you get anything done with him. If you ask twice the answer is usually no. Three times and it's still no, but the no takes a little longer to come out. Four times and he begins to think of it, and then five times and you get a yes. It works every time.

'He said that we could use transport to get people over to your village, and that we could collect people from Bury St Edmunds, as long as they don't mind travelling in a truck – not the normal transport for an orchestra! So that means that our driver can go up to Bury, collect the players, and then drive down to you. Once a month, though: no more, I'm afraid.

'I put a sign up in the Mess and on station notice-boards. We've had seven people say that they're interested and that makes eight, with me. So all you need to do is to get the word out in Bury – in the parish magazines perhaps, and then we're ready. I'm calling it La's Orchestra, by the way. Nice name!

'Have you found a conductor? Or will you do it yourself? Conducting doesn't seem awfully difficult to me – you just beat time and try to keep everybody together. Piece of cake, I would have thought.'

She smiled as she read the letter. The orchestra had been an impulsive idea on her part, and she had not imagined that it would get this far. But now it seemed to have taken on an energy of its own, and . . . well, why not? Why should she not have a little orchestra that would entertain the players even if it never entertained anybody else? People spoke about morale – there was a lot in the newspapers about that, and an orchestra would certainly help morale. That was what orchestras did. They played in the face of everything, as the orchestra on the *Titanic* did when it was sinking. It played. Well, we shall play while the country is fighting for its life. We shall play no matter what the enemy throws at us. They would prefer silence – so we shall answer them with music, or cacophony – it did not matter a great deal. As long it was not silence.

She put the letter aside but brought it out that evening when she was waiting for Feliks to arrive. He had said that he would be there at seven, but did not come until almost a quarter to eight, when La had been on the point of deciding that he would not be coming at all. She thought it unlikely that he had forgotten, and he seemed too well-mannered to stand her up. He had lost his way, perhaps, or there had been some crisis at the farm – the fox, maybe, attacking the hen house. But he did not do that in broad daylight; his raids came at night.

She felt uneasy, on tenterhooks; she paced about the kitchen and went out into the garden to look at the rows of potatoes she had planted in a dug-up section of the lawn. The garden was almost entirely given over to vegetables, now – a wartime garden in which flowers and shrubs took second place. But she could not concentrate this evening, and found herself looking anxiously down the lane for any signs of Feliks.

When he eventually arrived, she felt only relief.

'I'm very sorry,' he said. 'Henry cut himself. I had to make up a bandage. His finger.'

She winced. She had seen Henry fumbling with a vegetable knife in the kitchen. She asked how he was and was reassured that the cut was not too bad. 'I have told him that I can cut things for him,' said Feliks. 'But he is proud.'

'Yes. He does not want to be an invalid.'

He had ridden over on Henry's old bicycle, which La had seen stored in a barn, covered in cobwebs. She showed him where he might stow it, and took him into the house. 'It is very beautiful,' he said, looking about him. 'These houses in England are so beautiful. They are so peaceful.'

She led him into the sitting room. When she had first come to the house, she had found a bottle of Gerald's expensive sherry, which she now opened. She poured a small glass for each of them and passed one to him. He raised it politely, straightening up as he did so and then bowing slightly in her direction. The gesture seemed to her to be very formal, almost Prussian, but she remembered what Tim had said about his background. This was no ordinary farm worker; this was an educated man, a member of a landed family, for all she knew. Many of the Poles in their air force were from that sector of society, she had heard.

While they drank the sherry, they spoke about his cottage. He was completely satisfied with it, he said. It was heaven. 'I do not have to listen to other men snoring,' he said. 'That is bliss for me. Bliss.'

She asked him about his English. He had studied it at university level, he said. English and Polish literature. He found that languages came naturally to him, and that when the war was over, if Poland was still there, he would return to the university and complete the doctorate he had embarked upon.

'It must be strange,' she said. 'One moment you are studying for a doctorate and the next you are in the air force. And then you're digging ditches on a farm.'

'Everybody's life is strange. Everything is turned upside down in war. It is not strange.'

She read him the letter from Tim. 'He said that you play the flute. He thought you would be able to play in our little orchestra.'

Feliks was self-deprecating. 'Me? I am not very good. Not good enough for an orchestra.'

'There are orchestras and orchestras,' she assured him. 'Nobody in this one will be very good.'

'Even so, I have no flute. I'm sorry. I cannot.'

He moved the conversation on to another subject, and then they went through to the kitchen, where she had laid a gingham tablecloth on the table and place-mats at either end. She had made a salad using lettuce and radishes grown in her garden, and a sausage and sultana casserole. There were still sausages to be had, and she had prepared generous portions.

After the meal he looked at his watch. 'I will have to go now.'

'Yes, of course.'

There was still some light left in the sky, but he had brought a small carbide lamp should he need to cycle back through the darkness. She went into the garden with him and watched him mount the cycle. He smiled, and doffed the grey tweed cap he had brought with him.

He said, 'If you wish, I could look after the hens for you tomorrow. You could have a day off.'

She did not want that. She was used to her hens, and she felt responsible for them. She knew the fox and his ways; if her back was turned he would surely take advantage of that.

He cycled off, waving as he turned out of her drive and onto the lane, wobbling as he picked up speed. She stood for a moment and watched him before she went back into her house; he did not look back, and did not see her. The gingham tablecloth brought a touch of colour into the kitchen, a splash of red. That cheered the place up, but the house seemed empty now that he had gone, and for her part La felt ill-at-ease. She locked the back door and went into the sitting room. She had missed the main news bulletin on the wireless, but there was a later one that she just managed to catch. There had been further raids and the enemy had lost a substantial number of aircraft before they had been able to reach their targets. The voice of the newsreader was even; the voice of one who was used to the breaking of bad news.

She listened in a half-hearted way, before switching off. She wondered what he thought of her. It was difficult to read him, and she feared that his politeness was just that and no more: politeness. He had shown no desire to stay and chat after dinner, and it was difficult to see why he should want to get back to his cottage when there can have been very little for him to do there. He did not want to spend more time in her company; that was the only conclusion she could reach.

She turned out the lights and went into her bedroom to get ready for bed. There was a mirror beside her wardrobe, and she looked at herself in this. I am not attractive, she said to herself. Not really. I am just the woman who looks after the hens. If he wants anybody, then it will be somebody younger, somebody more appealing than I am. There are plenty of girls, and with most young men away, they were eager to meet any man they could. Feliks was good-looking; he would turn heads. He could have any woman; he would not be interested in me.

She sat on the bed and removed her stockings. She glanced again at her reflection in the mirror. There are ways of looking into mirrors, she thought, one of which is to open your eyes and see the person who is looking back at you.

Fifteen

It was Tim Honey who did most of the work of getting the orchestra together. La recognised this all along, and later she said, 'Tim, you may call this La's Orchestra, but it's really you who's done all the work.'

He was modest. 'Nonsense. It's La's Orchestra because it was your idea and you're the conductor. Enough said.'

But she was right about the work. After he had written the letter to La, it was Tim who was in touch with the vicar in Bury. He proved enthusiastic: 'Can't play a note myself, not a note. Can't sing either – if you came to evensong here you'd know all about that. But there are plenty of people here who would like to join.'

The plenty of people of the vicar's imaginings turned out to be seven, but four of them were strings players – three violinists and a cellist – and one of them was a reasonably strong player. The violinists were all women – two sisters, retired teachers, who lived together, and the almoner from the hospital. The cellist was a man, a youngish bank manager whose asthma prevented him from joining anything more demanding than the Home Guard. They were all enthusiastic and had time on their hands, and had no objection to making the short journey from Bury in the back of an RAF truck.

With the eight volunteers from the base, most of whom were wind players, the orchestra at least had a core. To this there were added two players whom La had discovered in the village – the postman, Mr North, who had an ancient set of drums in his attic, and his sister-in-law, who was prepared to assist him in the percussion section 'as long as North keeps me right on the rhythm'.

'I shall do that,' said La. 'I am the conductor. You watch me.'

It was Tim, too, who managed to get together the music to start them off. The Air Force, he explained, had a music department – bands and the like – and they were sympathetic. A crate of sheet music was dispatched and triumphantly delivered to La's doorstep by Tim.

'Everything we need, La,' he said enthusiastically as he dug into the music. 'Look. W.A. Mozart, no less. Arranged by J.M. Williams. We've got a J. Williams at the base. One of the catering officers. Different chap. And this stuff here. 'An Evening in a Viennese Café' arranged for school orchestra. Not bad. All the parts seem to be there. More than we need.'

They sorted out the music as best they could and chose a piece for the first meeting. La looked at the conductor's score and wondered how she would cope with the reading of so many parts simultaneously. 'Easy,' said Tim. 'Concentrate on one section and conduct it. The others will find their way.'

They met for the first time in mid-August on a Saturday afternoon. La was waiting for the truck to arrive, standing in the village hall with the postman and his sister-in-law. They had arranged the hall chairs in a semi-circle around a portable pulpit that they had borrowed from the church.

The truck arrived and disgorged the players. Three of the men from the base were in uniform, the others were wearing civilian clothes. A couple were officers, both navigators; the other men were ground crew, including the station barber, a thick-set man with a Cockney accent, who had with him a battered silver trombone. The navigators looked tired, and one stared out of the window while La addressed the orchestra, as if he was looking for something. Tim threw him a glance, and then looked at La, as if in apology.

They played for an hour. It was ragged and discordant. Two of the violins, La was sure, were out of tune, and she stopped half way through to try to get people in tune again.

'We sound a bit flat,' she said.

Tim laughed, and this released the tension. 'Does it matter?'

'I suppose not,' said La.

'It's not me,' said the postman, and everybody smiled.

At the end of the session there was a cup of tea. The village hall had an urn, which had been switched on at the beginning of the practice and was now just at boiling point. The postman's sister-in-law took it upon herself to make the tea, and to serve it, using a jug of milk which had been donated by Mrs Agg, who was a cousin of hers. Their instruments packed away, the members of the orchestra stood and drank tea together.

'Are we going to give a concert?' asked one of the men from the base.

'Of course,' said Tim. 'We are, aren't we, La?'

She hesitated. Tim looked at her expectantly. 'At Christmas,' she said. 'We shall give a concert at Christmas. Here in the hall.'

'And at the base too?' asked Tim.

'Of course.'

'"An Evening in a Viennese Café"?' asked one of the navigators.

'Pre-*Anschluss*,' said La. 'Yes. And then . . .' She paused. 'And then, at the end of all this, at the end of the war, we'll give a victory concert. That's what we'll start practising for. A victory concert.'

There was silence for a moment. The postman looked down at the floor. Then Tim cleared his throat. 'A good idea. Look out suitable pieces, La.'

There were murmurs of agreement.

As they prepared to leave, Tim turned to her and whispered, 'Yes?'

She looked puzzled. 'What?'

'It worked? Do you think it worked?'

La smiled. 'Of course it did. You heard it, didn't you? You could tell?'

The engine of the truck was running and the driver was waiting for him. 'I mustn't keep them. Yes, I think it's fine. And that business about being flat . . .'

'It's not our fault,' said La. 'We're in the middle of a war, aren't we?'

Tim chuckled. 'Of course. It's the war.'

'Well, there you are,' said La.

She helped the postman and his sister-in-law clear up. They stacked the chairs to the side of the hall, as the vicar had asked them to do, and the pulpit was left for the verger to collect the next day. The postman emptied the urn onto the gravel path at the back of the hall.

'That's it,' said La. 'That's it until next month.'

As she walked back to her cottage, Mrs Agg passed on her bicycle, heading back from the village. 'I heard you,' she called out. 'They all heard you down in the village. Came across lovely. Lovely sound.'

'We're not very good,' said La.

'Sounded fine to me. Tra-la-la!'

The farmer's wife disappeared down the lane, and La continued her walk. I have an orchestra, she thought. Other people have . . . well, they have what they have. I have an orchestra. It was a sobering thought, every bit as sobering as if one awoke one day to find oneself in charge of Covent Garden or la Scala. There were shoulders that bore those very responsibilities, of course, but they did not belong to a woman in her early thirties, who lived at the edge of a small village in Suffolk, and who each morning looked after hens.

The following Saturday, after attending early to the hens, La made the journey into Cambridge. There was a bus that stopped in the village and then went on to Newmarket, and Cambridge beyond. She caught this at ten in the morning and by noon she was in Cambridge.

As she began her journey the sky was clear, and the ripening fields made swathes of golden brown, criss-crossed by the dark green lines of the hedgerows. It had been a good growing season and crops both official and unofficial were in riot: banks of nettles had taken hold of some of the roadsides; even the trees themselves seemed to have spread their reach, now and then brushing against the roof of the bus. As the journey progressed, La watched the men and women boarding the bus. For the most part they were going to Newmarket or Cambridge, setting out to buy the bigger things that village stores did not stock: a dress to wear at somebody's wedding in the autumn; a pair of stout breeches for the winter. La looked at the faces. When she had first come from London, the people had seemed somehow different, their eyes brighter, their skin a different tone. She remembered what Rupert Brooke had written in 'Grantchester' about the characteristics of people from the various Cambridgeshire villages; such exaggerated, tongue-in-cheek nonsense, but concealing a truth: people were different in different places. In the small corners of Suffolk there were families that had not moved for centuries; of course they would develop physical characteristics that were typical of place. And with those physical characteristics went moral qualities. Determination, courage, a sort of native cunning: those crossed generations, La thought. It took centuries to breed an Agg, she said to herself; and smiled at the thought.

In Cambridge she alighted on Trinity Street. The University was still on summer vacation – *down* they called it – and the street was quiet. A middle-aged man, a college servant La thought, judging from his formal black suit, was walking a small terrier along the pavement; a couple of women, smartly-dressed and not much older than La, came out of Heffers. One was holding a book that she had just bought and was discussing it with her friend, who nodded agreement at what she was being told. La watched this wistfully; this was what she was missing. She might be in such company, talking about the latest novel, instead of tending to hens at Madder's farm and digging potatoes in what had once been a lawn.

She turned the corner. Paulson's Music Shop was exactly where the advertisement claimed it would be, next door to a high-quality butcher on the one side and an outfitter's on the other. Both the butcher and the outfitter were trying to make the best of a bad moment in their history, with more-or-less empty windows. The outfitter, though, had obtained an academic robe in bright scarlet and had rigged this up on one of their mannequins; it made for a bright splash of colour. The music shop, though, was not feeling the emergency. There were still musical instruments to be had, and the window boasted a small display of violins and violas, alongside a couple of ornate wooden music stands.

La looked in the window before going in. She had discussed with Tim what scores they might obtain – the crate of printed music from the RAF had its limitations – and she would see whether she could order these. In the advertisement she had seen, Mr Paulson claimed to be an expert in obtaining the unobtainable: she would now put that to the test.

Mr Paulson, who appeared from a back room in response to the bell triggered by the front door, was finishing a cup of tea. He put the tea-cup down, straightened his tie, and greeted La.

'Such a promising day earlier on,' he said. 'But now, look at that.' He pointed at the sky through the window; a bank of heavy cloud had blown up from the east, high cumulo-nimbus, purple with rain.

'Yes. It looks very threatening.'

'But,' Mr Paulson went on, 'we are not to be dispirited by such small things as the weather. Especially when there is so much else happening.'

La produced the list she had written out and passed it over to him. Mr Paulson took a small pair of unframed reading glasses out of his jacket pocket and placed them on the end of his nose.

'Rossini. Yes. Mozart. Yes, and yes. Yes. That, alas, that piece there, no. That is out of print as far as I know and these days ... It is more difficult to get things. People often don't answer letters because ... well, there are no people in the offices any more. Heaven knows what happens to the letters.'

'If you can get just half of my list,' said La, 'I shall be very happy.'

Mr Paulson nodded. 'That will be no problem.' He slipped the piece of paper into a drawer. 'This is a school orchestra, I take it?'

La shook her head. 'I suppose that you would call it a village orchestra.'

Mr Paulson was impressed. 'Admirable! There used to be village bands, but now people seem to have lost the habit of making music together. Even the bell-ringers are finding it diffi-cult to recruit, you know. We have a team in my own parish, but there are very few young people in it. Sad.'

La agreed that it was. Then, 'And I wondered about a flute. I wondered if you had any second-hand flutes in stock.'

Mr Paulson did not answer directly, but turned and opened a large drawer to his side. He reached in and took out a small box, covered in black leather. 'Now this is a very nice instru-ment,' he said. 'It belonged to a young man who was at Clare until a few months ago. He took a commission in the Royal Artillery and sold this to me before he left. He said that he hadn't played it since he left Harrow. He said that it would be better if it were to be used.'

He slipped open the catch on the side of the box and extracted the disjointed pieces of the flute. These he quickly fitted together and handed the instrument over to La.

'There you are,' he said. 'That's a lovely old flute. Rudall, Rose,

Carte and Co. You see, that's their stamp there. Theodore Boehm himself authorised them to make his system here in England. They also made an eight-hole system, as I'm sure you know . . .'

La raised the flute to her lips and blew across the mouth-hole.

'A very true note,' said Mr Paulson. 'Try it across the range. You'll see how sweet it is. Lovely action.'

La lowered the flute and handed it back to him. 'It's not for me,' she said. 'My playing is a bit rusty. It's for a man who would like to play in our little orchestra, but who doesn't have a flute.' She paused. 'He's one of those Polish airmen.'

Mr Paulson nodded. 'I see. Well, that's a nice thought. I'm sure that the young man who owned this would like to see it going to a fellow combatant.'

They discussed the price. La saw the ticket on the box – it was surprisingly expensive – but Mr Paulson quickly reduced it. 'For our Polish friend,' he said. 'And they have suffered so.'

She wrote out a cheque. Her account was flush with funds; Gerald had given her Richard's share of the family company in cash, and had been generous; she could live on the interest alone. There was nothing to spend her money on in the village, and funds had accumulated.

The flute, and such sheet music from the list as had been in stock, were neatly tied in a brown-paper parcel and handed to La. Then, with an anxious eye at the storm clouds, and with Mr Paulson's assurances that the other sets of music would be found if humanly possible, she left the shop and headed back towards Trinity Street. She looked at her watch. There was a further appointment in Cambridge, before she caught the bus home, and for that she would treat herself to a taxi.

* * *

As she stood before Dr Leontine Price's door, La thought: how many times have I stood here feeling slightly awkward about something? From her first visit to her tutor, summoned on the day after her arrival in Cambridge all those years ago, to her last visit, on the morning of her graduation, her encounters with Dr Price had been ones in which guilt of some sort or another inevitably seemed to play a part. In her first year she had always felt that the essays that she wrote for delivery to her tutor were not quite her best work; that there were insights that she had but could not quite express; that Dr Price would be bored by what she had to say. Later she had become more confident about her judgement – what she had to say about the Victorian novel, after all, was as *valid* as what any other undergraduate had to say, possibly even more so, as La knew that a number of the others who took the course with her were not above giving opinions on books they had not read. But Dr Price never gave the impression that she shared this view, and listened to La with a vaguely pained expression, as if she were keen to be some-where else, attending to more important things. 'As a matter of interest,' La wanted to say, but never did, 'you are being paid, are you not, to listen to me?'

Now she stood before Dr Price's door as a widow, the conductor of an orchestra, and the doer of war work, even if the war work in question was only the keeping of hens. Yet the familiar anxiety returned, and there was hesitation in her knock.

Dr Price was seated at her desk. La noticed, with some satis-faction, that the room was exactly as she remembered it. There was the chair in which she used to sit and read her essay to the tutor; there was the clock that, ahead of the church clock at Grantchester, stood always at five o'clock, and still did.

'Your clock,' she said, pointing across the room. 'Still at five.'

Dr Price looked up from the papers before her on the desk. 'Ah, yes. I must wind it. So here you are, Ferguson. Here you are.'

Yes, thought La, I am still Ferguson, I suppose.

'Stone now.'

'Of course. I'm sorry, but it's hard for me to keep up. I tend to think of people as who they were when they first came up. You're Mrs Stone. And Mr Stone, how is he?'

La looked at the woman she had come to visit. One of the reasons why people like that were the way they were was because people let them get away with it. Well, she would not. Not this time.

'He died, I'm afraid.' She surprised herself in the utterance; surprised that she could talk about Richard so dispassionately.

If Dr Price was taken aback, she did not show it. 'I'm sorry to hear that.' But she went straight on; husbands died, and sometimes, Dr Price felt, not prematurely. 'You must sit down, Ferguson. Usual chair.'

La looked about her. There was another chair, closer to Dr Price's desk. She chose that; and immediately felt petty. There was a war going on for the very soul of civilisation, and she was trying to avoid sitting in a particular chair.

'You must tell me what you're doing,' said Dr Price. 'The College newsletter lets one down a bit in that department. They're good on graduations and obituaries, but not all that informative on what happens in between.'

La smiled. 'And that's the important part, isn't it?'

'Indeed.'

There was a brief silence. Then La said, 'But what have you been doing? The usual?'

La looked at Dr Price, who held her gaze. 'I see.'

La knew immediately that Dr Price had understood her. The chair. The immediate turning of the question back on her.

The tutor waited for a moment. She ignored the question. 'It's good of you to come back. We don't really change here very much. Universities think in centuries, of course. If you go and stand in some of the older colleges – Peterhouse, I suppose, would be the case *par excellence* – if one stands and contemplates what those buildings have seen, then things are rather put in perspective. Our current difficulties will pass.'

'Our current difficulties?'

'The war. Hostilities. This business between men.'

La thought of her job with the hens. She thought of Tim and his talk of supplies. Petrol. Spare parts. She thought of the navigator who looked out of the window.

'I'm not sure that it's just between men.'

Dr Price waved a hand airily. 'Men have always fought. It's what they do. They jockey for position. Puff their chests up and strut around. Then, every so often, they unroll their sleeves and take a swipe at one another, just to establish the pecking order.' She paused. 'I find it very entertaining.'

La touched the fabric of her chair with her hand. It was a heavy tapestry. Roses. 'I'm not sure if what is happening in France is entertaining for the French.'

'France and Germany are old enemies,' said Dr Price. 'We must expect them to engage in these aggressive charades with one another.'

'And Hitler?'

'He is the worst sort of man, the very worst. And of course we have to do what we can to prevent him from invading this country. I wouldn't dream of saying otherwise. But he does rather illustrate what I said about male behaviour, does he not?'

Dr Price allowed a few moments for her observation to be absorbed. She picked up a piece of paper from her desk, folded it, and replaced it. In a moment of clarity, La remembered her doing that in their supervisions. She had watched her from the chair, wondering what the action showed about her reaction to the essay. Boredom, perhaps. Irritation?

'Are you involved?' said Dr Price after a while. 'Remember Thompson? Mathematician – quite a good one too. She was about your time, was she not? She's down in Buckinghamshire doing something very hush-hush. Shades of Mata Hari. I met her at the station the other day. She declined to say very much.'

'I remember her very slightly,' said La. 'Am I involved? Well, I suppose we're all involved, aren't we? I do some work on a farm.'

'Land girl?'

'Not quite. It's a private arrangement. I look after hens for a farmer. He's got bad arthritis, you see, and can't cope any more. I feed the hens.'

Dr Price nodded. 'You're busy.'

'And I have a village orchestra,' La went on. 'We have an RAF base nearby. Some of the men come and play music with us.'

It all sounded so petty. Hens. Village orchestras.

Dr Price looked at her watch, surreptitiously, but sufficiently overtly for La to see that her visit was over.

She rose to her feet. 'I've enjoyed seeing you again, Dr Price.' She paused. There was so much to say to this woman; so much that she had wanted to say over the years, but had never had the opportunity to do so. And even now, she could not bring herself to do it. But still she said, 'Tell me, Dr Price, what would happen, do you think, if Hitler came? What would you – and I mean you personally – what would you do?'

Dr Price uttered a sound that was mid-way between dismissal and irritation. 'Strange question,' she said. 'But don't worry, he's not coming.'

La wanted to say, 'Because there are hens and orchestras to stop him?' But Dr Price gave her no opportunity, even had she found the courage. The tutor stood up, sighed, and stretched out her hand for La to shake it. This, La knew, was a farewell that was not just for the moment, nor for the duration of the war, however long that would last.

Sixteen

She watched Feliks at work on the drainage scheme. Pott's Field stretched over several acres and it would take some time for the channels to be dug all along the edges and then led off downhill to the stank. And there were root systems to contend with – over the centuries the hedgerows and trees had consolidated their grip on the soil, knitting together in places, breaking up stones in the process; dying, renewing, creating a sub-soil through which the spade could cut only with difficulty.

La watched the work progress; it was painfully slow, even though Feliks was always working when she looked across in that direction; a tiny figure from afar, bent over the land. She kept about her business with the hens and then, when she had finished and had washed up in Henry's kitchen, she took a glass of lemonade to Feliks.

'You're spoiling him,' said Henry, half-joking, half seriously. He seemed vaguely annoyed, and La suspected that he resented the attention she was giving Feliks. Why? She thought that it was probably not out of any hostility to Feliks himself, whom he appeared to like, but out of jealousy.

'It's hard work. Really hard. Have you been down there? He gets thirsty.'

'There's water,' muttered Henry.

'But there's also lemonade.'

She found a recipe for lemonade that could be made without lemons, which had never been sold in the village store anyway. She made a quantity of this in the kitchen, not asking Henry's permission but just doing it; if he wanted her to work on his farm, then she would use his kitchen. She tested it: it tasted good enough to her, and Feliks liked it. He smiled when she told him she had made it herself. 'You're so kind to me,' he said. He was always telling her that she was kind to him, and she wanted to stop him, to say this is what she wanted to do.

Which was what? What was it that she wanted to do? She asked herself the question and could not think of any answer other than that she wanted to look after a man; it was as simple as that. Some deep instinct within her had asserted itself: an instinct to cherish another person, a man in particular. What would Dr Price make of that? She smiled. Dr Price had never looked after anybody but herself.

She found herself thinking of him a great deal. She thought of him as she cycled to the farm in the morning, wondering whether he would already be out in Pott's Field when she arrived at the farm. She thought of him in the evenings, when she sat alone in her house and listened to the news and the musical programmes. She tried to stop herself, but could not.

She asked herself whether he would have done this to her had he looked different, had he not had about him that unsettling male beauty, that glowing smoothness and harmony of feature. At first she thought yes, and then she thought no. And it was the no, she imagined, that was more realistic. Human beauty requires of us an intense response. We want to own the beautiful, we want to possess it. We wish that it would somehow rub off on us, simply by being in its presence. That is how she felt about Feliks.

He was polite to her, but that was all. He was a shy man, she decided, and that was why he seemed reserved. That would pass, she thought, when they got to know one another better, but she was not quite sure how to achieve that. There was the flute, of course, sitting there in her house, in its fine leather-covered box, and she wanted to give it to him. But she was nervous; it was a large present, and she did not want to smother him.

It took a week. Then he came into the kitchen when she was stacking eggs in the box that Henry used to transport them in to Bury. He used straw to prevent them from being broken; the dust from this would tickle her nose, make her eyes run.

She heard his voice behind her. 'You do not like that work. I could do it for you.'

She turned round, wiping at her eyes with the back of her hand.

'It's all right. It passes. The straw . . .'

He nodded. 'When I was a little boy I used to sneeze all the time in the summer. Then suddenly – just like that – it stopped. No longer.'

He moved past her and began to place the eggs in the box.

'Do you like your work?' he asked.

La sat down on one of Henry's rickety kitchen chairs. 'I've got used to it. I suppose that the hens and I have become friends, in a way.' She looked up at him, noticing for the first time that there was a scar under his chin, a thin line that had been neatly sliced into the skin, as if by a flourish of a pencil.

He fumbled with an egg.

'Careful. Henry gets very upset if I drop one. He shouted at me once. He said, "The Germans want you to drop those eggs."'

Feliks smiled. 'You could tell him it was me.' He paused. 'I'm not sure that he likes me anyway. It would be one more thing for him, maybe.'

La frowned. 'You think that he doesn't like you? Why?'

'The way he speaks to me.'

She thought about this. Henry had a grudging manner, but he was like that with everyone, La thought.

'I don't think he dislikes you,' she said. 'It's the way he is. Maybe it's something to do with his illness. He has a lot of pain, you know.'

Feliks nodded. 'Maybe. It can't be easy to be like that. His hands . . . I think that they must be very painful. But even so, I think that he does not like me because I am a foreigner.'

La was about to reassure him that this was not true, but she realised that it might be exactly the reason; that, or he was jealous of the attention that she gave to Feliks. But she could not mention that.

'I have something for you,' she said.

He placed an egg on the straw and turned to her. 'For me?'

'Yes. I've bought you a present. I think that you'll like it.'

He looked puzzled. 'But why? Why have you bought me a present?'

La shrugged. 'You're far from home. Who else is there to buy you a present?'

'But just because I'm far from home does not mean that you need to . . .'

La interrupted him. 'No. Of course I don't need to. But I have. It's at the house. My house. Perhaps you will come and fetch it.'

He came the next day. She was in her garden when he arrived, riding the old bicycle from the farm. She saw him from her bedroom window upstairs and she watched him as he walked across the gravel to knock at her door.

She had put tea in the pot and there was a small plate of freshly baked scones.

He gestured to the scones. 'You should not have bothered . . . just for me.'

'I had some flour. If you don't use it, it gets weevils.'

He looked confused, and she explained. His English was good, but there were words now and then that defeated him. One would not learn weevils.

She went out of the room to get the flute. When she came back in, he sprang to his feet.

'This is for you.'

She handed him the box.

He looked at her.

'Go on. Open it. Please.'

He eased back the catch and pushed open the lid. She noticed that his hands were trembling slightly.

'Oh. Oh.'

He looked up at her again. She found it hard to read his expression.

She smiled. 'You did say that you played the flute, didn't you? Well, there you are. A flute. Try it.'

He shook his head while he eased the flute joints into place. He muttered something, which she thought was in Polish. She hardly heard it.

'I believe it's a good one,' said La. 'Not that I'm the best judge of these things.'

He raised the flute to his lips. La saw the concentration, and she knew, even before he drew breath, that he would play it well.

After a few notes, a scale, he lowered the flute and shook his head. 'It is so kind of you,' he said. 'But I cannot pay for this. I do not have the money.'

He began to disassemble the flute.

'No,' La protested. 'Don't do that. You don't have to pay for it. Don't be so silly. It's a present. I told you.'

'But I can't accept a big present like this. A small present, perhaps . . . but this is a very big thing. It's a good flute. And I can't pay.'

It was not going well. She had anticipated some awkwardness over her gift, but not this. She had not thought he would insist on paying for it.

'Listen, Feliks. This is a present from me to you. I'm giving it to you because you are far away from your home. Maybe you have a flute back in Poland – I don't know. But I want you to have this because we are in the same war together.' She sighed. She did not think that she was convincing him. 'All right. When the war is over, pay me then.'

He stopped disassembling the flute. 'At the end?'

'Yes. Whatever will make you happy.'

He thought. 'All right. But in the meantime, you must let me do something for you.' He gestured behind him, out of the window. 'Your garden. I could help you with your garden.'

She felt the release of tension, and laughed. 'My garden? Yes, that would be very useful. Such as it is, now that I have all those potatoes.'

He was staring out of the window. 'You can make a garden around the potatoes. I could make it beautiful for you. Next spring you would see the difference.'

She accepted. She felt gratitude at the thought that he would be there, in her garden. That was what pleased her.

'And you can play in my orchestra. It's not much, but we don't have a flautist.'

He made a gesture of modesty, of reluctance. 'I will not improve it. My reading of music is rusty.'

'Anybody would improve us,' said La. 'Even a rusty player. You must.'

He picked up the flute and slipped the joints together again. She could tell that he held it with love, and that convinced her that she had done the right thing.

'Go on. Why not play it? Play anything that comes to mind. Something Polish, perhaps.'

'I had an uncle who was a very good player. He played beautifully. My uncle in Frank . . .'

He broke off, his comment left hanging in the air. La looked down at her shoes. One of them, the left one, had a small crust of mud on the tip. She had not noticed it. She moved her other foot to dislodge it. Perhaps she had misheard.

He did not play the flute, but twisted its sections apart, put them away quickly and then rose to his feet, suddenly formal again.

'I'm very grateful for this gift,' Feliks said.

She forced herself to smile. 'Good.'

'I must go now,' he said.

'Of course.'

She watched him from the window, her thoughts in confusion. She saw him walk down the gravel drive towards the bicycle. Then suddenly he turned round and looked back at the house. La took a hurried step back so that he should not see her at the window. But he had spotted her, she thought, because his eyes had gone to the window at which she had been standing.

She crossed to the back of the room and pushed the door shut. Then she sat down, in the chair that he had occupied. She noticed that he had left a small canvas shopping bag on the floor. She hesitated for a moment, and then picked it up and looked inside.

What did I expect? she asked herself. Something more than this? There was a small onion at the bottom of the bag; a small, scruffy onion from which the first layer of skin had begun to peel; that was all. She replaced the onion and put the bag on the dresser. She would take it back to him tomorrow, at the farm. She moved back to the window and gazed out at the field on the other side of the road. What had he said? That he had an uncle in somewhere that sounded like Frankfurt. It was a perfectly innocuous comment: anybody might have an uncle in Frankfurt – if that is what he had said; the husband of his aunt, for instance – a Polish woman marred to a German; there must be many such marriages when countries neighbour upon one another. Poles and Germans spilled across one another's borders, and where exactly these borders should be was one of the issues behind the war anyway. Feliks could be a Silesian German who saw himself as a Pole; such people presumably had to make a choice, and many of them must have thrown in their lot with

Poland rather than Germany. But would a German-speaking Pole have an uncle in Frankfurt? Quite possibly: having an uncle in Frankfurt did not make one a German.

She persuaded herself. It was nonsense. The problem with war was that it made us all so suspicious. We saw things that were not there; we imagined an enemy behind every innocent bush or tree; saw clouds as veils for bombers, and death; saw the world as a place of dread and distrust; saw an honourable Polish airman as a fifth columnist, or even something worse.

She would not be part of that narrow climate of distrust and suspicion; that was simply not the way that she thought. Feliks was an exile, far away from home, friendless, and dependent on the charity of others; she would not be the one to challenge him, to make him feel that he was the subject of narrow mistrust, from her, as much as from everybody else.

The decision made, she did not allow herself to think about the matter again. And the next day, when she saw Feliks again, it was as if nothing untoward had occurred. That proves it, thought La. That proves that whatever it was that I heard was nothing of any significance. She made him his lemonade and took it down to Pott's Field. He thanked her and told her that he had tried the flute out when he had got home the previous evening. He would never be able to repay her, he said; never, as it was far too good an instrument for him. She said, 'But you're going to do my garden for me, remember?'

He nodded. 'Of course, I'll start that. I'll come tomorrow. After work.'

'Bring the flute. And you will play in my orchestra?'

He hesitated for a moment. His eyes, with their rather unsettling lucent quality, were upon her. 'You really want me to?'

'Of course I do.'

'Then I shall do what you want.'

He arrived at her house the next day, in the late afternoon, as he had promised. She walked round the garden with him and discussed what needed to be done. They would grow more vegetables, because that was what everybody was being urged to do.

'So there should be no flowers in wartime?' he asked.

'Not so many, perhaps. But there should always be room for some flowers. Even in wartime.'

He reached down and picked a weed that had intruded on a flower bed. 'Just as there should always be room for God, even in wartime. Some people in Poland, you know, said that he had gone away. Some of them were Jews who felt that they had been abandoned by God.'

'One might understand their feelings. Everybody else seems to have abandoned them. Looking the other way.'

'Not in this country,' said Feliks. 'You have been kinder. You have never allowed that. Some people, maybe, have said cruel things. You had your fascists too. But not in the same numbers as back there. These things go back a long time.'

Cruel things. She liked his turn of phrase. It did not dress anything up. This war was about hatred, she thought; hatred and cruelty on a massive scale.

'We can't afford to be without God,' Feliks continued. 'Even if he doesn't exist, we have to hold onto him. Because if we don't, then how are we to convince ourselves that we have to go on with this fight? If you take God out of it, then right and justice become small, human things. And weak things too.'

La thought about this. He was right, perhaps, even if she did not feel that she needed God in the same way Feliks seemed to need him. She would do whatever she had to do – even if it was for the sake of simple decency. You did not wipe a child's tears because God told you to do so. You did it because the tears were there.

He worked in the garden for two hours before she called him in for a cup of tea. They sat together in the kitchen and then La suggested that they play a duet together; she had looked out some music.

He was better than she was; far better. But he was a considerate partner, and they reached the end of the piece together. He laid down his flute.

'You are every good.'

She laughed. 'I'm not.'

'No, your playing has expression. It is very good.'

They played another piece. At the end of that, he looked at his watch. 'It's getting late.'

She did not want him to go. She almost said, 'Stay with me and have supper. I have enough food here.' But she did not. It was not a good idea, and she should not allow herself to become involved with this man; she would only make a fool of herself, as he would not reciprocate. If you are going to love him, she said to herself, it is going to have to be from a distance. Secretly.

Seventeen

It was autumn. Feliks had finished Pott's Field and had brought in Henry's harvest. The toll on the hens had been heavy: the foxes, perhaps sensing that their human adversaries were pre-occupied, had bred enthusiastically and their cubs had proved cunning – and hungry. With Henry's summer crops in, there was not much for Feliks to do on Madder's Farm, and after a call from an official from the Ministry of Agriculture – a visit in which voices had been raised – he was allocated to help over the winter on a pig farm several miles away; he might come back in the spring, but no promises were made. Henry accused Feliks of requesting the transfer and did not believe him when he protested that it had not been his idea.

La drove Feliks to his new cottage, his possessions packed into the back of her car. Everything he possessed had fitted into two trunks and a battered cardboard box; she found it difficult to take in that this could be all that a man might own in this world; if it was indeed all that he owned.

She asked him about it as they drove over. It was a Sunday

afternoon in late November. A cold fog had drifted in from the east that morning and had lingered, a white shroud over the landscape, dusting the hedgerows and the branches of the trees with rime. Here and there, stark against the white, a winter crop made a carpet of dark green. She thought it strange that war should go on when nature wanted things to stop, to pause, to sleep for a while.

'What did you leave behind?' she asked. 'You've never told me much about your life . . . before. Did you lose a lot?'

His hands were clasped together on his lap. He opened them. There was an intimacy to their conversation in the car, an intimacy that seemed lacking elsewhere, lacking, even when they'd played a duet. When they spoke at the farm he was always on the point of doing something, on the point of going some-where. He did not answer for a few moments. But then he said, 'Leave behind? Nothing very much. A car. An elderly mother. A sister who is a nun.'

She reflected on his answer. It was a life condensed into telegraphese. And her own life in such terms – what would it be? An unfaithful husband who died. A house in Suffolk. A rag-bag orchestra. A vegetable garden.

'You lived in a city?'

He stared out of the car window; wiped at the condensation with his sleeve. 'Yes. Although my mother lived in the country. A small estate. Not very big at all, and with quite a few debts. My father was never very good at such things.'

La felt satisfaction that she had guessed correctly. A gentleman. 'I could tell . . .'

She noticed him tense up as she began her response. 'You could tell what?' he asked.

'I could tell that you came from a certain background.' She paused. 'Well, to put it very directly, I could tell that you were a gentleman. Not . . .'

He laughed. 'Not a peasant?'

'That's not a word we use in this country.'

He seemed intrigued. 'You have no peasants? What about Henry? Is he a peasant?'

It was La's turn to laugh. 'Henry, a peasant? That's very amusing, Feliks. No, Henry would not describe himself as a peasant.'

'But would you describe him as one?'

'Certainly not. I told you: we don't go in for peasants here. We have yeomen, of course. But that's something quite different. To call somebody a peasant would be insulting. People are sensitive about that sort of thing.'

'In Poland it's not shameful to be a peasant. It's an honest thing to be.'

La thought that was right. After all, everything above the rank of peasant involved some pretension, some claims of superiority over others. But be that as it may, Henry Madder was certainly not a peasant.

'He's quite well-off, actually,' she said. 'Henry. I think that he's got money tucked away in that house of his.'

'That's what peasants do with money,' said Feliks. 'They tuck it under the mattress. Everybody knows that – and that includes thieves!'

'In Warsaw, were you . . .'

He held up a hand. 'Krakow. Not Warsaw.'

She corrected herself. 'Were you at the university in Krakow? Tim said that you were studying.'

'I was. And then I went off to join the air force with some friends. It was just the thing to be in the air force. We Poles used to think that the cavalry was the place to be – it was very dashing, very romantic. You have no idea what the Polish cavalry was like. But the air force was even more so. My friends led a very romantic life. Lots of parties and aerobatics.'

Parties and aerobatics: La smiled at this. And then, she assumed, everything had suddenly become very serious.

'And now this,' she muttered.

'What?'

'I mean, this . . .' She took a hand off the wheel and waved it at the fields. 'Suffolk. A pig farm. A funny little orchestra with a lot of people who can't play very well.'

'Maybe,' said Feliks. 'But then you can consider anybody's life, can't you, and find things in it that are very ordinary. And in war time, I think, the important thing is to be alive, don't you think?'

La suddenly thought of Richard. Yes, what Feliks said was right, even if . . . but there was no more time to discuss it. They were near the pig farm; they could smell it on the wind. She glanced at him quickly, and then looked back at the road ahead. She felt confused: she wanted to be with him, she wanted to be close to him, but she did not want to be rebuffed. If he did not reciprocate her feelings, and she thought that he did not, then she would make sure that she did not have those feelings. It was as simple as that. She was certainly not going to be one of those women who pined for an inaccessible or indifferent man; she would not be hurt again.

She helped him with his suitcases and the box; his meagre possessions that looked all the more pathetic when stacked outside the door of his new home; a life in two suitcases and a box. She remembered the words that had impressed her so deeply at that first funeral she had attended, that of an elderly homosexual uncle who had been shunned in his life and wept over in his death: *It is certain that we bring nothing into the world and it is certain that we leave with nothing.* So all the rest, even this small collection of possessions, was temporary. And yet so strong was our sense of ownership, even for our limited tenancy, that there were those who were prepared to kill others for what they had, just as there were those who were prepared to give their lives in its defence.

The cottage that he had been allocated by the farmer turned out to be no more than two rooms added onto the end of a tackroom. La could smell the leather of the harnesses through the thin walls; the sweet smell of dubbin, the mixture of horse-sweat and oil. Everything was run-down: the grubby windows let in very little light, and there was a pervasive feel of damp in the air.

La was indignant. 'They can't expect you to stay here. They can't. Look. Look at the patches on the wall. That's damp. See? If you put your hand there you can feel it.'

Feliks looked about him. 'It's a roof over my head. I can't be fussy.'

La snorted. 'I can. I'm going to talk to the farmer.'

He took hold of her arm. It was the first time he had touched her. 'Please don't. I'll tidy it up. I'll heat it and the damp will go away. Everything will be all right.'

She was reluctant, but he insisted. He would not let her stay to help him clean and tidy the place, and so she left him there in her anger and drove home. She had wanted to say that he should come and stay with her; she had more than enough room in the house, but she did not know how to put it; whatever she said, she suspected that it would sound like an invitation to be something more than a lodger.

She asked herself whether that was what she wanted, whether she would like Feliks to be her lover. She was not sure; the war made everything different. If she became involved with him, she would have to accept that he could go away. He came from a different country, from a different world, and sooner or later he would want to go back to that world. She belonged in England and her sense of that belonging was all the stronger now that England was under such threat. I love this country, she thought; I love everything about it; its lived-in shabbiness; its peculiar, old-fashioned gentleness. I love it.

Feliks did not come from that world, and yet he seemed so at home in it. He would never be accepted by the people among whom La lived, and who had accepted her; and yet they were kind to him. He was a stranger and they had taken him in.

The thought came back to her as she drove back along the winding lanes: what if the stranger who had been taken in was not what he claimed to be? What if the man who accepted the kindness of those who took him in, secretly contemplated the defeat of that very kindness? She shook her head, as if to rid it of the unwelcome thought. She had set those doubts to rest some months ago, and she did not want them to recur. Feliks was exactly whom he claimed to be. He was a Pole who had lost the sight in an eye in the defence of his country, and, indirectly, of hers. That was all there was to it.

Feliks joined the orchestra. On the first occasion he played he was shy and did not stay for the cup of tea that everybody else took at the back of the hall once they were finished. La looked for him, but he was gone. 'Who is that flautist?' asked one of the violinists from Bury. 'That good-looking man?'

'A Polish airman,' La replied.

'He can certainly play, can't he?'

'I think so.'

In December they performed for the first time. Their first concert was in the hall they practised in; the village was abuzz and turned out in force, even Agg and Mrs Agg, who sat in the front row and clapped loudly even after the applause from the rest of the audience had died down. The second concert was at the air base, where their final piece was interrupted by the sound of aeroplanes taking off. Tim could attend for only half of the concert; he was fetched out to deal with some emergency and did not appear again until the end, when tea and cake were served by two women volunteers in light blue air-force overalls.

Tim asked her about Feliks, and whether he had settled in at the pig farm. 'I think so,' she said. 'If you thought Madder's Farm was tough, then you should see where he is now. The farmer is a perfect tyrant, and there's not much difference between Feliks's accommodation and the sties the pigs live in.'

Tim laughed. 'He's resilient. All these Poles are.' He paused. 'You found a flute for him?'

La looked across the room, to where Feliks was standing, talking to the two sisters from Bury. She wondered whether there was something else behind the question, but decided there was not. She told him about the trip to Cambridge and the discount the man in the music shop had given her.

'I'm glad,' said Tim. 'And I'm glad you're keeping an eye on him. You know, he wasn't very popular with a couple of other Poles we had at the base. They seemed to be a bit . . .'

La waited. Tim made a face, as if to portray stand-offishness. La relaxed.

'Keeps himself to himself?' She wondered how she could put it to Tim that it was probably a social matter. The problem about being direct, was this: Tim himself was not a gentleman. That did not matter to La, who was largely indifferent to such distinctions – or at most observed them wryly. But it was difficult, she thought, to explain to one who was not a gentleman that others might dislike another because he was.

'Not so much that,' said Tim. 'It's just that they seemed not to take to him. It's as if they were a bit suspicious of him.'

La lifted her tea-cup to her lips and took a sip. She felt cold inside.

'But you never know with these types,' Tim continued. 'Look at the French. They're always bickering with one another. You'd think that they'd all agree to get behind de Gaulle, but not a bit of it. Maybe it's the same with the Poles.'

La hesitated. Perhaps now was the time to say something to Tim. She could tell him about the Frankfurt incident, but what exactly would she say? That she thought that Feliks had let slip that he had an uncle in Frankfurt? Did she really have to bring up something as slender as that?

She swallowed hard. She had her duty. 'How well do you know him?'

'Dab?'

'Yes.'

Tim shrugged. 'Quite well, I think. I ended up looking after him, as you know, arranging things. He was a bit of a lost soul.

I suppose I got to know him better than some of the others because he speaks such good English. It's always easier when you feel that the other chap is taking in what you're saying. He understood everything – even jokes. Sometimes you tell a joke to a foreigner and he looks at you blankly. That can be a bit tricky.'

La said that this was not what she had meant. 'About his background? About where he comes from?'

Tim looked at his watch. 'I'm going to have to dash. We've got rather a lot on our hands, even if it is Christmas.' He drained his cup. 'Dab's past? Polish Air Force. Wormed his way in with our boys after he was picked up in Romania. That's where their air force fled after the Jerries and the Russians gobbled their country up. Didn't I tell you about that? Poor chaps. Most of them went to France first, of course, but some of them had the foresight to see that France would fold like a pack of cards. He didn't intend to stay there long – and he was shot down on his first sortie. Just like that. He came here to carry on the fight. That, as you know, was not possible.'

La nodded. She had heard that before, when Tim had first mentioned Feliks. She wanted to know about what happened before France. 'So he would have been checked up on?'

'Of course. Everyone is. There's a Polish command that vouches for people. They know who's who.' He paused. 'You've got doubts about him?'

'I just wondered . . .'

Tim smiled. 'I really don't think that Dab's anybody to worry about. He's very much a gentleman, you know.'

La broke into a smile.

'Have I said something funny?'

'No. No. Not at all.' She did her best to hide her relief. It was just as she thought: she had been imaginative because she was living in times when the imagination could so easily be over-fired. War made heroes of some, she thought, but for most of us it made us frightened – and suspicious of our fellow man. She would not be like that, no matter how unpleasant life became. She would not.

Over the next few months, La's orchestra, which she had thought might grow weaker, actually strengthened. Word got round, and new players asked to join. There were more people from the base and more, too, from Bury. In the spring they gave another concert, this time in a church in Bury, and the local newspaper reported it in glowing terms. 'They may be amateurs,' the press report read, 'but they are determined. And what spirit they have! This is what Hitler hasn't taken into account: the determination of the ordinary people of these islands to get on with their lives in spite of everything that he throws at them. Watch out for La's Orchestra, Herr Hitler!'

Feliks settled into his new job on the pig farm, and reported to La that his rooms were no longer damp. The pig farmer, he said, was a generous man, in spite of having a reputation for meanness in the area, and the work was rewarding. He had managed to save much of his pay, as the farmer fed him and apart from his visits to the local pub at weekends there was nothing for him to spend his money on.

As he had promised, he came to work in La's garden once a week. It was spring now – they were on the cusp of summer – and the herbaceous border Feliks had planted was beginning to get some colour. He had cut back some of the shrubs which had got out of control and he had expanded the vegetable garden.

La now grew carrots, kale, lettuce and beans as well as her large crop of potatoes. Feliks announced that he would try to get hold of Jerusalem artichokes and rhubarb, both of which could be left to get on with growing and required little attention. 'Soup and pudding will be taken care of,' said La. 'Thank you.'

'But what about the course in between?' he asked.

'Henry's hens provide me with eggs,' said La. 'If an egg is cracked, we can't sell it, but it never goes to waste.'

Food: people now thought about it all the time, with a dull, nagging obsessiveness. La knew that she was lucky: her vegetable garden provided her with more than enough staples, and the eggs made a big difference. But what people wanted, as always, was what they could not get: meat, butter, sugar, coffee. The forces did better, of course, and pilots never went without. One of them, who played in her orchestra, brought her chocolate from time to time and slipped it to her after the rehearsal. She made it last, breaking off half a square after dinner each night and letting it dissolve slowly on her tongue. When hostilities ceased – as they had to do – she imagined herself eating large bars of chocolate in their entirety, gulping them down and unwrapping another bar while her mouth was still full with the previous one. If gluttony was a deadly sin, then it was only such in peace-time; in war the deadly sins were permitted; surely they were. People took pleasure where they could find it, and with gratitude – chocolate, love, anything that used to be in plentiful supply but which was now hard to find, or rationed.

Eighteen

It was a Saturday in August. Feliks had been working in the garden and La had fallen asleep in a deck chair under the willow near what remained of her lawn. She awoke suddenly and found that he was sprawled out on the grass beside her, his feet resting against the first hummock of the potatoes that had replaced the lawn. At first she thought that there was something wrong; that he had become ill from exertion in the heat, but then she noticed that his eyes were open, staring up at the sky, and that protruding from his mouth was a blade of grass that he was sucking. He was lying to her right; his left side towards her. She noticed the profile of his nose; it was perfect, she thought. It was what made him so handsome.

'You know,' she said. 'If somebody came and took away your nose, you'd look very different.'

He took the blade of grass out of his mouth. 'What an odd thing to say. Anybody would look different.'

She laughed. 'Yes. Sorry, I was just thinking aloud. But it's more true with some people than with others, don't you think?

I know of some people who would look the same, with or without their nose. Mrs Agg, for example. Her nose . . . well, her nose is neither here nor there, if you ask me.'

He continued to stare at the sky. 'You are very strange. They say that English people are peculiar, but you must be very peculiar to say things like that.'

La was silent for a moment. It was rare for them to talk in this relaxed way; it meant nothing, she knew, and the spell would soon be broken. He would get to his feet and carry on with his work in the garden – or suddenly pack up and leave, as he often did. But for now she was enjoying the moment.

'Don't Polish people say silly things from time to time?' She glanced at him. 'Or are they too sad?'

He reached out to pluck another blade of grass.

'We are not always sad. We were very happy when we got our freedom back in 1918. We went mad with joy. The whole country.'

'And that was the last time anybody was happy?'

He seemed to think for a moment. Then, 'When we showed the Russians that we would fight for our freedom and when we beat them. We were happy then. That was 1920.'

'And now?'

There was a silence. La shifted slightly in her chair and looked up through the leaves of the willow to the clear sky above.

'Now we're too busy,' he said. 'We're too busy to think much about whether we are happy or sad. We've got one thing on our mind. To get the Germans out.'

La nodded. 'Why are they there in the first place?'

'Because they are. They've invaded.'

'But why?' La pressed. 'How would a German explain it? What would a German say?'

'We would say that the Poles could not run their own affairs. That everything was chaos and that the German invasion was the best thing that had happened to Poland. That is what they would say.'

La lay quite still. She was staring up through the leaves as he spoke, and she continued to do so. There was a bird in the branches, almost directly above her, as if unaware of her. She watched his tiny, jerky movements. She did not say anything.

Feliks said something else – something about Russia – but she did not hear it. *I cannot let this pass*, she said to herself. *I cannot ignore it now.*

She sat up. 'Feliks,' she said. 'Do you know what you just said?'

He did not move, and La remembered that he might not be able to see her. He was lying to her right, with his left side towards her, the side of his bad eye. She moved her hand slightly, in a wave-like movement. He did nothing. He could not see her.

'About Russia?' he said. 'About Stalin wanting his revenge?'

She felt her heart hammering within her. 'No. Before that. I asked you what a German would say about Poland, and you said *We would say . . .*'

He remained still. 'No, I didn't say that. I said something else.'

'But you did. You said it.'

He sat up, quite abruptly, and La gave a start. He turned to her. 'I said that the Germans would say something about chaos and bad government, if they told us what they really think. They do not think that the Poles can run a country, or deserve to do so.'

He rose to his feet. 'I'm going to tie those beans,' he said. 'Then I'm going to have to go.'

'I must pay you,' she said. After the first few months, when he insisted that he was paying for the flute, La had taken to giving him money for his work in the garden. He had been reluctant to accept it, but she had insisted. Now she got up out of her deck chair and went into the house to fetch the coins from her purse.

Inside, she stopped for a few moments in the corridor. Perhaps it really was a slip of the tongue; he's speaking a foreign language, after all, even if he speaks it very well. That must be it. *We* and *they* are easily confused; anybody might make such a mistake.

She took the coins out to him. He seemed to have forgotten the incident, and talked to her about the four rows of beans of which he seemed very proud.

'You will have a very good crop,' he said. 'You wait and see.'

La listened to a story on the radio. It was about a woman who lived in a small town in Kent who took a lodger, a commercial traveller. The traveller had a leather suitcase in which he kept his samples; he sold brass fittings to hardware stores, and the case sometimes made a clinking sound when he set it down. He was a good tenant; he paid the landlady his rent every Friday morning and he was always neat and tidy. On Sundays he went by bus to a Catholic church before he came back for lunch with his landlady. He often had a small gift of something for her – a jar of marmalade, a small parcel of lamb chops. He was married, he said, but his wife was living in Belfast, where she was looking after her infirm mother. They would get together again when the mother was no more: she could not last forever, he said.

The landlady found one evening that her lodger had left his sample case on the landing. She picked it up and took it to his room. She knocked, but he did not reply, and so she opened the door gently. He was sitting at the table near the window, writing something in a book. When he saw her come into the room, he closed the notebook and stood up. He seemed very uncomfortable that she was holding the sample case, and he took it from her quite roughly. She was surprised, but understood that men sometimes became short when they had been working too hard, and were tired.

The lodger kept odd hours, but that was not unusual for a commercial traveller. He went off to the railway station and took trains to various parts of the country. He had clients all over England, he said.

He seemed to have no friends, or none that she knew about. He came from Manchester, he said, but he had no family up there any more. He was a loner, she thought; she had had lodgers like that before, and they were no trouble.

La listened to this. It was a trite story and she knew exactly where it was leading. People were always being told to be on the look-out, to be careful of what they said and to whom they said it. The landlady would come into the room and discover a transmitter, or a code-book perhaps. It was all too obvious.

And it was uncomfortable. She turned off the wireless and went to stand by the window. It was afternoon and the shadows were lengthening. That evening they would have an orchestra rehearsal, and she had matters that would occupy her mind. She was copying out a part for one of the trumpeters – slow, laborious work that she did not enjoy – and she should be doing that rather than listening to the radio. Ridiculous story – like a simplified morality play for the unsophisticated. Did they really want to have everybody looking into everybody's business, just in case . . .

After a few minutes she went back to the wireless and turned it on again.

'. . . at his trial,' said the voice. 'The landlady was there, and one or two intelligence people who had been involved in the case. The judge said very little. The case had been one of the worst he had seen; the information sent back to Germany could have cost the lives of many innocent people. There was a sentence provided for by law and that was the sentence that he now felt he must impose.

'They took him away. He showed no emotion, even when his landlady looked at him from the public benches. He gave no indication of recognising her. He said nothing.

'In prison he refused food, right up to the time that they took him from his cell. His legs failed him at the end, though, and they had to carry him to his death; he died a coward. Afterwards he was buried in an unmarked grave. They never knew his real name, but they were sure that he was an Englishman.'

That was the end of the story. La turned away from the wireless in her irritation. Why had they called him a coward? She thought that he must have been brave, not a coward at all, taking all those risks and then saying nothing. That was brave, even if he was on the wrong side, on the side of darkness. And anybody's legs would fail them if they were made to walk to their death. What did they expect?

She sat down. She felt an emptiness, a rawness within her. She loved Feliks; she admitted that to herself now. *I love him*. It was an unreciprocated love, yes, but it was love nonetheless. She did not want him to die, to be carried to his death like the man in the story. Yet just as she admitted to herself that what she felt for him was love, so too she had to admit to herself that her duty was clear: this war was about evil, and the innocent could well be the agents of evil. Misguided people no doubt believed in Hitler and his cause; might even think they were doing the right thing. Feliks could be one of those; or he might be an uncomplicated patriot, for whom it was not a question of loyalty to Hitler and the Nazis, but to Germany itself. People said that there were officers in the German army who were in that position; men with a sense of personal honour, torn between loyalty and disgust. Oh Feliks . . .

She had to speak to Tim, not in the indirect way that she had on that previous occasion, but openly and unambiguously. He was rational and level-headed; a balanced man. He would assess whether what she had to say amounted to any sort of evidence at all, or whether there was an innocent explanation.

She telephoned Tim, who was not at his desk. The flight-sergeant who answered, whom La had met in making arrangements for the orchestra, said that he would pass on the message to call her back. Fifteen minutes later, La received the call.

'I suppose you've heard,' Tim said to her before she could say anything.

'Heard what?'

'They've arrested Feliks.'

Nineteen

She did not care that it would make her late for the orchestra. It was not an afternoon for cycling, the strong wind in her face making progress slow, but she had pedalled that route to Madder's Farm so often before that she could do it virtually without looking where she was going. She had been there that morning for the hens and had left at eleven; everything had been normal then. She had exchanged a few words with Henry when she was stacking the eggs, but only a few words. His pain was worse; she could tell that since he was moving slowly, and he was always more taciturn when he was in pain.

She found him in the kitchen, sitting at the table, a half-drunk cup of tea in front of him. He looked up at her, eyes narrowed.

'So, you've heard.'

She took off her scarf and tossed it down on the table. 'What happened?'

'He stole my money,' he said. 'He stole all of it.'

'When?'

He took the cup in his right hand, carefully inserting one of his immobile fingers through the handle. 'This afternoon. Lunchtime. I was down at Pott's, and when I came back up I saw somebody cycling away from the house. It was him. I called after him, but he paid no attention.' He paused. 'Then I went in and something made me check the . . . the place where I keep some money I have. It had been taken. All of it. Near on eight hundred pounds, if a penny. Eight hundred.'

La did not like the way he was looking at her. It was as if he felt triumphant; having suspected all along that Feliks was a thief, now he was being proved right.

'But were you sure it was him?' she asked.

'Yes. Of course I was. I know that man as well as you do.' He looked at her. 'Well, maybe not quite as well as you do . . .'.

La ignored this. 'Maybe he came to see you. Maybe the money was already gone.'

Henry eyed her. 'Wasn't gone yesterday.'

'Well, it could have happened any time from when you last checked up on it. Where did you keep it?'

'Cupboard.'

'Which cupboard?'

'Cupboard in the sitting room. Round the front.'

La thought for a moment. 'That's a room you hardly ever go into, Henry. The door's always closed there. You know that.'

He stared at her sullenly. 'So? Money's gone. He was here.'

In the past La had noticed that when Henry decided that something was the case, then it was not easy to shift him. He was doing it again. Feliks had been on the farm and the money was gone. The two facts seemed to him to be inextricably linked.

She tried again. 'All that I'm saying is this, Henry. You don't know when the money went missing. It could have been last night. You never lock your doors, do you? No, you don't. I know that you don't.'

He shook his head. 'I would have heard somebody. If somebody came in last night I would have heard him. I'm a light sleeper. Always have been. I would have heard somebody downstairs.'

'No, you wouldn't necessarily. People can be very quiet. You sleep upstairs, don't you? You do.'

He contemplated this for a moment before he spoke again. 'Anyway,' he said. 'Percy Brown's been down here. He said he was going over to arrest him at Archer's place. So that's it. And all I want to know is – when will I get my money back? They'll find it in his room, likely enough.'

La sighed. 'You could be wrong, Henry. Have you thought of that?'

'Ain't wrong.'

'Well, anybody can be wrong, you included. And if you are, then you've accused an innocent man of being a thief. How would you feel if you were accused yourself of stealing something and you hadn't? Can you imagine how you would feel?'

'Haven't stolen anything,' he said. 'Not me. So your question makes no sense, La. And here's another thing. Four eggs broken this morning. You've got to be more careful, La. Four eggs wasted.'

The trip to Madder's Farm made her arrive ten minutes late at the village hall. They were working on an arrangement of 'Brigg Fair' that had been sent from Cambridge, with a recommendation by Mr Paulson. It was on the outer edge of their abilities, and they were struggling. The percussion was all wrong, and there was a new violinist from one of the nearby villages who was very rusty with the instrument. La glanced at Tim, who shrugged, but smiled encouragingly. It was not going well.

La remembered the words. They came back to her as she struggled with the music: *It was on the fifth of August, the weather fine and fair/Unto Brigg Fair I did repair, for love I was inclined.* She thought: to repair somewhere with love. To repair somewhere with love. *I took hold of her lily-white hand, O and merrily was her heart/And now we're met together, I hope we ne'er shall part.*

She looked down at the music on the stand in front of her. She tried to keep time, but she lost the place and had to turn a sheet quickly. The orchestra continued, although one or two of the violins faltered. Tim looked up at her sharply. She concentrated on the music, but the words returned to her mind. Brigg Fair. *I hope we ne'er shall part.* One did not dare hope that; not these days, when people were thrown together in the arbitrary confusion of war and parted as easily and as quickly as they met. Yet people loved one another; in the interstices of all this, love was possible.

La put down her baton. She could not continue, for the tears she had fought to suppress now overcame her. She turned away, so that people might not see her cry. She put her hands up over her face.

One of the sisters from Bury was beside her. 'La, dear. La.' There was an arm about her, and she was led to a chair at the side of the hall.

'I'm sorry. I'm just all over the place tonight. I'm sorry.'

'Hush. Hush. You don't have to say sorry. There, La. There.' She leaned forward and whispered, 'It's Feliks, isn't it, La? It's Feliks?'

Tim was standing behind the woman from Bury. 'Is there anything . . .'

'She'll be all right.'

La looked up at Tim. She saw that the orchestra had broken up and people were packing their instruments away.

'Tim, I'm so sorry. I should have asked somebody else to take over tonight.'

He nodded to the woman, who moved away to let him forward. She threw an anxious glance at La.

La looked up at Tim, who had reached out to take her hand.

She had a handkerchief and wiped at her eyes. The tears had stopped, but her cheeks were still moist. 'Can I talk to you in private?'

He nodded. 'Of course.' He looked over her shoulder. 'Look, the truck can take everybody home. I've got my car this evening. I'll drive you back to your place.'

They did not wait until the hall had been closed off, but went out to Tim's car and drove back down the lane. Tim was quiet in the car, although he said, 'It's been a difficult day for you. I can tell that. I was pretty taken aback myself.'

In the house, she put on the kettle and they sat down at the kitchen table.

'So,' said Tim. 'Dab has been arrested. A nasty business.'

She took a deep breath. 'It's not that. Not the theft.'

He was puzzled. 'He's been arrested for something else? Where did you hear that?'

'No, I don't mean the arrest at all. I want to talk about something else. I think that Feliks may be German.'

For a few moments Tim said nothing. Then he reached into a pocket and took out a packet of cigarettes. 'I see.' He extracted a cigarette and tapped it against the table. La watched him. 'And why do you think that?'

She told him about the slips – the uncle in Frankfurt and the *we* rather than *they*. He listened carefully, and raised an eyebrow over the *we*.

'Does that sound fanciful to you?' La asked. 'I was listening to a story on the wireless the other day about a landlady . . .'

He smiled. 'Oh yes, I heard that. I was in the mess having a cup of tea and it came on. I listened to the whole thing.'

'It was silly,' said La. 'Very melodramatic. But it made me think.'

'So you think that you and I are in the same position as that landlady? And Dab is our commercial traveller?'

It sounded ridiculous, put that way, but that, she supposed, is what she thought. She nodded. 'Something like that.'

Tim lit his cigarette. La did not like the smell of tobacco, but tolerated it. Everybody smoked now, it seemed, and one could hardly object to the RAF doing it.

'All right,' he said. 'We can look into it. My first reaction, though, is that there's nothing to it. Remember that lots of Poles are German-speaking. Of course Hitler has grabbed many of those and made them join his army. But there must be some who are not too keen on the Nazis.'

She listened. Confiding in him had been cathartic, and now she felt there was nothing more to say. She had decided it was her duty to betray Feliks, and now she had done it.

Tim looked at her quizzically. 'I take it that there's nothing else. You didn't see him do anything that made you wonder?'

She shook her head. 'Nothing.'

'Well, then, there's a chap at the station who handles this sort of thing. He can get somebody down from London.'

It seemed so bleak. Somebody down from London would interrogate Feliks. And if they found out that he was an enemy agent, then they would execute him. War was like a game; one side did this and the other side did that. There were the rules, and these stipulated that those who played without uniforms would be shot out of hand.

Tim blew smoke into the air. 'I wouldn't worry, La. It's highly unlikely that Dab is anything other than what he says he is. I like him. I don't think I would ever feel like that about a spy. I like to think I could tell.'

She thought about this for a moment. What he said was reassuring, but there was still the question of the theft. They had not talked about that. La raised it now, and Tim shook his head vehemently.

'Can't be,' he said. 'I just can't imagine him taking anything. He's not a thief, he's . . .'

'A gentleman?' La supplied.

Tim laughed. 'Exactly. I told your policeman – what's his name?'

'Percy Brown.'

'Yes, I told Percy Brown it was highly unlikely. He telephoned me because Dab had given my name when he was arrested. He said I would speak for him. So this Brown chap phoned and I said that I didn't think it very likely that Dab would steal anything.'

La remembered what Henry had said about the possibility that the money would be found in Feliks's room. She asked Tim about this.

'Brown said he took a look and there was nothing there. He implied that they didn't have much proof, and that at the moment it was just the farmer's word.' He paused. 'I think they'll release him, although the intelligence people might want to hold onto him for a little while before they do that. They might take him down to London for a couple of days, but I suspect that he'll be back. He'll be playing the flute again in your little band, La. Don't you worry.'

Twenty

The following day, when she had finished with the hens, La cycled over to the pig farm. She had seen Henry briefly that morning, but they had not spoken very much. He had made some remark about the weather, and she had given a vague reply. There was still a gloat in his eye, and if he was waiting for a chance to discuss Feliks's arrest, she would not give him that.

The pig farmer was grooming his horse when she arrived. He was a tall man, with heavy eyebrows and an aquiline nose. Feliks had said that he was a keen horseman, which somehow La did not associate with pig-farming, but here was the evidence.

He did not seem surprised to see her. 'You're the woman who looked after him?' he asked. 'The woman with the garden?'

She nodded. 'Yes. He helped me in the garden.'

The farmer continued with his grooming, running the brush down the animal's flank. He slapped at a fly that had alighted on the horse.

'A nasty business. Percy Brown was round here this morning, with him.'

'With Feliks?'

'Yes. They were in a car. I've never seen old Percy Brown drive a car, but he had somebody from Bury at the wheel, I think. They came to let Feliks get his things. He's cleared out now.'

The farmer looked at La and saw the effect of his words. 'Sorry. I can see you're a bit upset about this. Nice fellow, Feliks. And not a thief, I'm pleased to say.'

La caught her breath. 'No? Percy Brown said that?'

The farmer took a small metal comb out of his jacket pocket and began to scrape the impacted horse hair from the grooming-brush. 'Yes. Percy Brown took me aside and said there was no real proof that he had pinched Henry Madder's money. Miser that Henry is. Eight hundred quid? Did you hear that? It'll be one of the gypsies down at Foster's. Light-fingered lot.'

'So why didn't they let Feliks go?' She knew, of course, but she had to ask.

The farmer started to brush the horse again. 'Who knows? Something to do with being Polish perhaps?'

She waited to hear from Tim, thinking that he might telephone her. But no word came. Feliks had been arrested on a Monday, and had been driven away on Tuesday. It was now Friday, and La thought that if Tim had not phoned her by mid-afternoon, then she would get in touch with him. She did not like to disturb him at the base; they needed to keep their lines open and private calls were discouraged. She was also unsure if he would know anything; but she had at least to ask.

La attended to the hens, which took her more than three hours, as there was cleaning out to be done. Henry was watching her from his kitchen window, but when she went to stack the eggs in their box he was nowhere to be seen. She decided that he must have been told that Feliks had been cleared of the theft, and imagined he would be sulking. He would not have changed his mind about Feliks's guilt; she was sure of that. She could just hear him saying, 'Percy Brown got it wrong again!' He had little time for Percy Brown, she knew, and he would presumably have even less time for him now. A long time ago there had been an argument between the two of them, and Henry's resentment had simmered. The country was like that; some arguments went back over generations; disputes over fields and boundaries, livestock, marriages.

Back at the house, La tried to busy herself with domestic tasks. She did the laundry – in her distraction she had put it off over the last couple of days, but now she was running out of clean blouses and had to do it. She scrubbed and applied washing blue, and thought of Feliks in London, facing his accusers. She wondered whether they would present him with the evidence against him – such as it was; if they did, then he would know who had betrayed him.

At noon, with the washing pegged out on the line, she decided to go over to Mrs Agg's. She had harvested carrots and had too many. Agg liked carrot cake, according to Mrs Agg, and La knew that their carrots had been destroyed by pests that year. Carrots would be welcome.

Mrs Agg was in her kitchen. She took the carrots gratefully. 'Carrot cake,' she said. 'Agg loves it.'

La smiled. 'I know. You told me that once. There'll be more carrots. I've got lots.'

Mrs Agg went to a cupboard and took out a small packet. 'These are dates,' she said. 'For you.'

'How did you get them?' La asked – and immediately regretted the question. One did not ask about luxuries; one was simply grateful for them.

'I had a spot of chicken on my hands,' said Mrs Agg. 'And Jimmy Mason had some dates that he'd got from heaven knows where. He's not too keen on dates and so . . .'

'Of course.'

La slipped the dates into her pocket and watched as Mrs Agg put the kettle on the range. Then she saw the new gramophone at the other end of the room.

It was standing on a table, with a small stack of records at its side. La looked enquiringly at Mrs Agg. 'That's new.'

Mrs Agg glanced in the direction of La's gaze. 'That ? Oh yes, that's Lennie's. He loves music – always has. Bands. That sort of thing.'

La rose and crossed the room to stand beside the gramophone. The turntable was covered with a rich, red baize; the head of the arm was shining silver. 'His Master's Voice,' she said. 'This is very nice.'

She picked up the record on the top of the pile and read out the label. *Billy Cotton and his Orchestra* and underneath *Ellis Jackson Plays.* 'Lennie's?'

Mrs Agg nodded. 'He plays them again and again. It drives poor Agg up the wall.'

La turned round. The door that led from the kitchen into the yard had opened and Lennie had entered. He looked at her quickly, and then looked away again. La smiled at him and greeted him, but got only a curt nod in return. She noticed that Lennie was carrying a large parcel wrapped up in brown paper and tied with white string. She did not want to stare, but her eyes were drawn to the parcel and then to the leather jacket that he was wearing. The jacket was clearly new; a soft brown leather with sheep's fleece lining at the collar – the sort of jacket that pilots wore.

Mrs Agg intercepted La's glance. 'Lennie, Mrs Stone has brought us some carrots for carrot cake. Isn't that kind of her?'

Lennie said something that La did not quite catch and then hurried through the door that led into the rest of the house.

'It looks as if Lennie has been shopping,' said La. 'His new gramophone. And that was a very nice jacket he was wearing.'

Mrs Agg's eyes narrowed. 'Lennie's not a great one for shopping,' she said. 'No man is. But he saves up his money and every so often he has a little spree.' She spoke firmly, as if to dare La to contradict her.

La did not say what she was thinking. The coincidence was just too great. Henry Madder loses eight hundred pounds and Lennie Agg goes on a shopping spree. There might be no connection, but La remembered something Dr Price had said in Cambridge: 'People always deny that *post hoc* means *propter hoc*. But so often, Ferguson, it does, you know. It just does.' She could not remember in what context Dr Price had made this remark, but it had lodged in La's mind, largely because she had used it that very evening when dining in Hall. There had been a heated debate on T.S. Eliot and modernism, and she had entered the conversation with the observation that one had to be careful not to conclude that *post hoc* was *propter hoc*. There had been a silence: nobody could see the relevance of the remark, but nobody wanted to be thought stupid. The emperor's new clothes are often insubstantial, but, as in the story, there are few who want to be the first to ask a gauche question.

After her cup of tea with Mrs Agg, La walked back down the lane sunk in thought. It was just before one in the afternoon, on a still day. Although it was late autumn, the sky was filled with clear blue light, and was cloudless, apart from several faint lines and whirls of vapour, fast dispersing, high above her – where aeroplanes had briefly danced, one with another in anger, or so she assumed. A year ago this choreography would have been part of the desperate fight that they knew would determine their fate; now it was merely part of a battle that seemed set to continue for years, as the last one had, until one side bled the other to exhaustion. There could only be one outcome, of course, and everybody, it seemed, knew what that would be; nobody doubted but that Hitler would be crushed, but it was taking so long, and was such a dispiriting business. What would people remember of this time, La asked herself. The drabness? The fear? The sheer human loss? Or would they remember the camaraderie, the sense of national purpose, the conviction of being engaged together on something immense and dramatic?

She felt somehow dirtied by what she had seen in the Aggs' kitchen. There was Lennie, able-bodied and every bit as fit to fight as that boy from the village who had been torpedoed last week and whose mother she had seen sobbing in the post office, comforted by the postmaster's wife; there was Lennie, who had taken advantage of Henry Madder, a virtual cripple, and stolen his eight hundred pounds. Mrs Agg must have known that Lennie had suddenly got his hands onto money, with his new gramophone and his leather jacket, and that large parcel, whatever it had contained. She must have wondered where he got it; there would be no secrets in a family like that, all living cheek by jowl in that small farmhouse. La could have told her about the money, could have mentioned the theft, but did not, because just to mention it would have amounted to an accusation, and one could not fall out with neighbours in the country. They relied on one another. She and the Aggs had to live together, and if she denounced Lennie as a thief that would be impossible. Besides, he was, she thought, dangerous. He had broken into her house before, and he would do so again if he thought that she had informed on him. But she knew that this was how evil prospered; this was how appeasement made tyrants confident. One turned a blind eye; it was the same with countries, as it was with people.

She made herself a cup of tea and took it out into the garden, to drink it there. The ground was hard with the cold; the clear weather had brought frosts at night that had frozen the crenellations of the mud into tiny, brittle fortifications. The mounds where she had planted potatoes were wavering lines, miniature hills and valleys marching across the garden's landscape. This was her plot of earth, the bit that she would have to die to defend, if it came down to it.

She suddenly felt defeated, and lonely. She had not realised how important were the visits that Feliks had paid to her garden. She had watched him working; they had talked. He knew what she was saying; he thought the same way: it was a question of simple *understanding* of the world. He understood. He was a friend – that was all – a friend whom she had come to love, but who would never love her back in that way. She could accept all that, but she would still miss him, she would miss him so acutely.

She did not think that she would see him again. Whatever happened to him, he would be unlikely to come back. They had taken him to London and he would be swallowed up by the city, carried away somewhere on the shifting tides of war, just one more displaced person in an ocean of human flotsam.

And it was now, as she walked slowly about her garden, that she decided that she would give up her orchestra. She no longer had the spirit for it. She wanted simply to withdraw to her house, to read, to listen to the wireless, to struggle with her vegetables. She would look after the hens – perhaps seek out more war work of that sort – but she would keep to herself, in the little world that she had made for herself, where she could be safe.

But she knew that there was something she must do. The whole point about this war was that it involved doing the right thing. She had to speak to Percy Brown.

She found him in the police house, in his stockinged feet, while Mrs Brown fried something on the stove; sausages, La thought, from the smell.

'My tea,' he said, almost apologetically. 'Not that there's much meat in sausages these days. I sometimes wonder what they put in them. Do you know?'

'Bread, I think. Bread and dripping. A bit of gristle.'

He grimaced. 'I shouldn't have asked. But they smell nice.' He looked down at his feet. 'I must put on my shoes.'

She held up a hand. 'Don't bother on my account. I won't keep you long.'

He gestured to a chair, and then sat down himself. 'Well, I assume it's about that man. That Pole. I've had no news of him, I'm afraid. They took him to London for questioning and they haven't let me know what happened. They never do, these hush-hush types. They don't trust anybody. Not even policemen.'

'It's the times we live in,' said La. 'It makes us all suspicious. The powers that be encourage it, don't they?'

Percy Brown agreed with this. 'Quite right, Mrs Stone. Quite right.' He raised an eyebrow. 'So there we are. We'll just have to wait until he comes back – if he comes back, should I say.'

'It's nothing to do with his being questioned,' said La. 'It's about the theft of Henry Madder's money. I understand that you decided there was nothing to link Feliks to that.'

'That's right. Henry Madder just caught a glimpse of a man on a bike. I pressed him on this and he had to admit he couldn't say for definite it was the Pole. And if you get a witness like that in court, the case usually collapses. Magistrates don't like that sort of thing. It wastes everybody's time.'

'Of course. But what about information that somebody's suddenly begun spending money very freely? If that sort of information comes in just after a theft, what then?'

The policeman frowned. 'It can do. Thieves often give themselves away like that. We had a man over in Bury who bought a car two days after a house-breaking. He didn't have a penny in the bank until then. Then he goes down to Ipswich and comes back with a nice little Austin. A bit like yours, actually. That was his undoing.'

There was a noise from the kitchen. A door closed, and the smell of sausages faded. Percy Brown leaned forward. 'You've seen somebody spending money?'

La swallowed. 'Yes.'

'Who?'

La held the policeman's gaze. If she had been a suspect, she would have found his eyes the most difficult of all. They were the eyes of a countryman, but there was a knowingness about them.

'Lennie Agg,' she said quietly.

She had not expected her words to have quite the effect they had. Percy Brown sat back in his chair, as if he had been pushed by an unseen hand. It was a few moments before he spoke. 'What did you see?' he asked.

'A new gramophone. And a leather jacket. And he had something else in a parcel. All wrapped up.'

He considered this quietly. 'I see.'

La felt that she had to explain. 'Lennie never gave any sign of having much money. His clothes . . . Well, he dressed very simply, mostly in working clothes. Even on Sundays, nobody saw him in anything special. Then suddenly this very expensive leather jacket appeared. And where would you get something like that these days? You'd have to pay through the nose on the black market. And the gramophone – it's an HMV – must have been very expensive. There were records too . . .'

Percy Brown was looking away. She could tell that what she had said was not welcome. Again, it must be a question of her having an unfounded suspicion.

She felt foolish. He must think that she was one of those ridiculous people who imagine all sorts of crimes; first, the man breaking into her house; then Feliks; now Lennie. He might be wondering when she would denounce him himself. After all, being a policeman would be perfect cover for anything.

'The only reason I mention this,' she said, 'is because I feel sorry for Henry. If Lennie has stolen his money, then you might be able to get it back before it's all spent. It's not easy for me, you know, to come to you and accuse my neighbour's son. You do realise that, don't you?'

He turned to her again. His expression had changed; it was

more closed now. 'Yes, I realise it, Mrs Stone. And I'm not criticising you for coming to me. It's just that I know that Lennie Agg, whatever else people may say he is, is not a thief.'

'But how can you be so sure?'

'Because he's my nephew,' said Percy Brown. 'And I've known him since he was *that* high.'

Twenty-one

It was two days before Tim came to see her. He came un-announced, at a time convenient for afternoon tea, which they drank in the sitting room, where La had treated herself to a small coal fire. It was the warmest room in the house, anyway, at that time of day, when the afternoon sun, if it shone, painted light on the floor and walls near the French windows.

Tim looked tired. 'We've had a beastly time of it,' he said. 'We've lost more crews than we can afford. Far more. And I'm having difficulty getting supplies that I used to get more or less automatically. There's some chap in the Air Ministry who seems determined to thwart me. I think it's personal.'

La looked sympathetic. 'Wish for his promotion. Then he can go and make somebody else's life difficult.'

Tim smiled. 'A nice tactic, La. One wishes for the promotion of one's enemies and feels good about one's charitable thoughts. And all the time . . .'

'Exactly. I've often noticed how there are people who always talk about doing the right thing. But when you look closely at

207

what the right thing is, it happens to be what's in their best interests anyway.'

'Human nature.'

La nodded. 'That's what they say.'

She looked at Tim. His face was drawn, and there was a pallor about him that she had not seen before. 'You're really tired, aren't you?'

He rubbed his forehead. 'Yes. But I'm alive. When I look at the list of names – the list of chaps we've lost – that brings it home to me. I'm not on the list.'

She reached across and poured him a cup of tea. 'You need a break. Can't you get some leave? Even a few days.'

He shook his head. He told her that he had applied for a long weekend to visit his wife in Cardiff, but his request had been turned down. He had even arranged the transport – a plane was going over there and they could take him – but it had made no difference. 'So I'm stuck. But . . . I suppose I can take a few hours to practise for the Christmas concert.'

La hesitated. It hardly seemed the time to mention her decision to stop the orchestra, but she feared there would never be a right time.

'On that,' she began, 'I've been thinking and . . . well, I feel that I've done everything I can with the orchestra. I thought I might stop.'

He stared at her. He was aghast. 'Stop the orchestra?'

I have the right to do this, she thought. 'Yes. We've been going for quite some time now. And . . . and I just don't know. I feel there's not much point to our carrying on doing the same old thing. Struggling through our somewhat limited repertoire. Not playing all that well. It's been fun, but . . .' She struggled to identify what it was that she wanted to say. 'I'm tired, I suppose. It's been fun, but you can't carry on indefinitely doing the same old thing, can you?'

He picked up his tea-cup and drank from it, watching her over the rim. Then, putting down the cup, he leaned forward. 'No, La. That's where you're wrong. We have to do the same old thing. We have to.'

'Why?'

He leaned forward even further, and took her hand. The gesture surprised her, and she wanted to withdraw it. But she could not; he gripped her. 'Why? You ask why? Because your orchestra, La, stands for everything that we're doing. We meet once a month and play because that's what we do. It shows anybody who cares to look that we are not giving up. And none of us can give up, can we? If we give up what we're doing, then everything's lost.'

She looked down at the floor. He was still holding her.

'Believe me, La,' he went on. 'Believe me. Your little orchestra means a lot to every one of those people playing in it. It means a lot to the chaps from the base. It means a lot to the sisters from Bury, to that old fellow who plays the tuba, to everyone, La. You are one of the things that are keeping us all going. Don't you see that, La?'

He let go of her hand and sat back in his chair. She looked at him, and their eyes were upon one another. She saw a tired man who sent other men to their deaths in great, lumbering planes; he saw an attractive woman, who was lonely and upset, and exhausted and dispirited by looking after hens and digging up potatoes.

He transferred his gaze out of the window. There was sunlight on the few lavender bushes that had survived the vegetable campaign. The grey-green foliage was briefly touched with gold.

'Oh my God, La,' he said. 'It's so damned hard. It really is. I know I shouldn't be defeatist, but we're on our absolute uppers. And it goes on and on. Maybe we should just . . .'

'The Americans might come.'

He shook his head. 'Do you really think so? We can't assume anything, you know.'

It was a while before she responded. She closed her eyes, and the thought came to her: defeat. She had heard about the *exode* in France over that terrible June; a Frenchwoman whom she had met in Bury had told her about it, in vivid detail. Of the families aimlessly wandering along the roads of rural France, fleeing the Germans; of the young women who covered themselves in Dijon mustard so that the Germans who raped them might be stung; of the young men being rounded up and taken off in trains; of the abandoned harvests and the empty towns. It might not be exactly the same, perhaps, but it would not be dissimilar. 'No,' she said. 'You're right. We've got no alternative but to carry on. We – you and I – can sit here and have our doubts about everything, but we can't let people see that, can we?'

'No. I suppose not.'

'And if the orchestra grinds to a halt, then people will know that we're giving up. They could think that, couldn't they?'

He smiled. 'It could get back to Churchill. Somebody could whisper to him, *Bad news, sir. We've lost La's Orchestra.*'

They both laughed.

'More tea, then?'

He accepted the offer, and she poured the tea into his cup.

'You'll have been thinking about Dab?' he asked.

She looked up sharply. She had not wanted to press him, in case he did not want to talk about it. But now he told her. 'I managed to get through the impenetrable barriers of the counter-espionage people. I happen to know somebody in London who does something in that department. He made an enquiry and let me know – off the record.'

She held up a hand. 'You don't have to tell me if you'd rather not.'

He shook his head. 'It's all right. It's not going to make much difference to the price of fish – or the war effort. Dab is in the clear. A *bona fide* Polish airman who had an unequal brush with the Luftwaffe in France and ended up here. As I always thought. Nothing untoward at all.'

She put down her cup. Her relief made her feel shaky.

'So he's coming back?'

Tim sighed. 'Sorry, La. But no. They've found some work for him in Cambridge. They needed somebody with languages – which Feliks has got. You know he's fluent in German and French as well as English? That sort of chap is very useful and so at long last they're going to be using his talents. Listening to radio traffic or something like that. Anyway, he'll be happy to be back in the fray. No more pigs.'

La's voice was quiet. 'No. No more pigs.' She waited a moment or two. Then she asked, 'Have you got an address for him? Do you know exactly where they've sent him?'

'Not the first clue,' said Tim. 'It was enough of a breach of security for him to tell me even that much. He couldn't say more.'

'Of course not.'

'Frankly, I'd say that he's disappeared for the duration, and . . . That's one of the wretched things about this whole show. All this not knowing where anybody is or what's going on. It's like being in a forest with a candle.'

She was distracted by the metaphor. Tim occasionally came up with expressions that did not quite fit. She pictured herself in a wood, with a candle. '*How far that little candle throws his beams,*' she mused.

He stared at her. 'What?'

'Shakespeare. You know how you remember bits and pieces? That's one that I always remembered. *The Merchant of Venice. How far that little candle throws his beams/ So shines a good deed in a naughty world.*'

'I see.' He paused. Shakespeare. He had a vague sense that Shakespeare came into what they were all doing; somewhere, in a way of which he was not certain. Somebody had said something about that on the wireless the other day, but it had gone in one ear and out the other, he thought. 'You're going to miss him, aren't you?'

She closed her eyes. 'I will. Yes, I'll miss him. I'll miss him an awful lot . . .'

'I'm sorry, La. I'm sorry about all of this. This wretched war. Everything. Maybe at the end of it all, he'll . . . he'll come back here.'

She did not think that likely. 'I doubt it.'

They sat in silence. Then Tim looked at his watch, and frowned.

'I'd better go. I'm on duty again in an hour.'

La rose to her feet. 'One last thing. Do you think he knows that I was the one who mentioned his . . . his slips of the tongue?'

Tim was not sure. 'Maybe. It depends on the interrogators. I imagine that they usually protect their informants, but then they may ask things that make it pretty obvious who's said what.' He stopped, and put a hand on her shoulder. He was like a brother, she thought. 'Are you worried? I don't think he's the sort to hold a grudge, if that's any help.'

The next day, when she had finished with the hens – the fox had learned to leap up into the laying boxes and had taken two overnight – she found Henry struggling to fix the latch on a gate. With his arthritic hands it was difficult to use a screwdriver and La gently took the implement from him and quickly effected the repair.

'I could do it,' he muttered. 'But my hands are bad today. Thank you, La.'

She looked at him sympathetically. 'You're doing well in the circumstances. Lots of people would have given up.'

'We don't give up,' said Henry. 'My dad didn't. He had the same thing. He never gave up.'

'Good. That's the spirit.'

She wiped her hands on the sides of her breeches; the screwdriver handle had been greasy. One of Henry's geese waddled past them and inspected them casually before continuing her journey.

'She's going to make somebody's Christmas,' said Henry. 'Look at her. Fattening up nicely. Getting ready for the big day.'

They began to walk back to the farmhouse, where the eggs were to be stacked before La left.

She chose her moment. 'I've had news of Feliks,' she said, once they were in the kitchen and Henry was putting on the kettle.

He was about to place the kettle on the range, and his hand stopped in mid-air before he lowered it. 'Yes?'

'Yes. Are you interested?'

He shrugged. 'Don't think much about him.'

La had not expected this. 'But you think he stole your money. Surely you . . .'

'No. Not any more.'

She stared at him. 'You do know that Percy Brown let him go?'

He stood with his back to her, watching the kettle. 'Knew that. He told me himself. Cycled out here and told me. No evidence, he said. Never liked him, that Percy Brown.'

'But he cleared Feliks. So that's that, isn't it?' She paused. She felt anger rising within her. Henry clearly felt no guilt about Feliks, and this appalled her. She would stop doing his hens; she did not have to stay. 'And you might think about saying sorry to him, you know. Not that you'll be able to find him.'

Now she added, although she did not know why; he did not deserve it. 'And I have an idea who took your money, if you're interested.'

He turned round to face her. He was smiling. 'Nobody,' he said. 'Nobody took it. It was in the other cupboard. Got a bit mixed up. It's all there. Every penny.'

She did not drink tea with him, but attended to the stacking of the eggs in silence. He watched her from the other side of the room, and although she tried to ignore him, she was conscious of his gaze.

'You're not cross with me?' he asked.

She did not reply.

'La? You're not cross, are you? I really thought it had gone. I looked and looked. But I had forgotten, you see, that I had moved it. It's easy to make a mistake, La.'

She sighed. 'All right, Henry. All right. I'm not cross with you.'

'Good. Careful with those eggs now. The shells get very brittle, you know, round about this time of year, when the hens are hungry.'

Twenty-two

'During war time,' remarked one of La's friends, much later, 'women receive offers. Later these offers seem so much less frequent.'

'What a peculiar thing to say!'

'But it's true, La. I really think it's true. Look at us. Look at both of us. How old were you when it started? You must have been about the same age as me – late twenties? Twenty-eight? Twenty-nine?'

'Twenty-eight. I was thirty-four when it finished.'

Her friend smiled. 'And you didn't meet any men? Right next door to an RAF base? What about that band of yours?'

'It was an orchestra.'

'Orchestra, then. Somebody said that you had air force people in it. You must have met bags of men, La. Nice ones, too. Americans. You could have ended up in New York . . .'

'I did meet men. But remember, I was a widow. I didn't feel that I wanted to get involved. It was such an odd time. There were one or two, yes. One, I suppose. A man who played the flute in the orchestra. A Pole.'

'Tragic. What they put up with.'

'Yes.'

'Tell me about him, La. Would you?'

I don't really know how to put it. You know how sometimes you meet somebody and you know that this person is going to be more than a mere acquaintance – you just know that. It's difficult to put one's finger on why you feel that – perhaps there's some form of chemistry there – not sexual – just a chemistry of friendship, if there's such a thing. That's how I felt about this man, Feliks. I just felt that.

Remember that I was widowed very young. In fact, I had already been left by Richard when he died. That was such a strange marriage. He had more or less pestered me into marrying him in the first place – he proposed after we had known one another for hardly more than a month. You know how it was in those days – you got married very early because that's the way it was. People expected it of you, and then you came to expect it of yourself. That was the way it was.

Do you remember Dr Price? Did you know her? We didn't really see much of one another when we were at Girton, did we, you and I? Of course I had just gone up when you were about to graduate, and so it was inevitable that we didn't get to know one another all that well. But you do remember Price, don't you? She was not at all keen on men – the female equivalent of some of those bachelor classicists in places like King's or Trinity who would run a mile rather than talk to a woman. Dr Price used to talk about the tragedy of her girls who went off and got married more or less immediately after finishing at Cambridge. She hated it. She said most of us would be unhappy. She revelled in that prediction; she loved news of divorce.

And she was right. Of course some were happy, but I think they were the minority. Most of us just made do. We worked at our marriages. We put up with unfaithfulness and unreason-ableness and seven-year-itches and all that. And we were unhappy.

You may think that's a bit cynical, but there we are. That's what I felt. Richard went off with somebody else and left me. Then he died. I was pretty confused, as you can imagine. I had fallen in love with him after we married – a dependence that you suddenly find has settled on you like a blanket you can't kick off. Well, I felt that. And so I felt terribly let down. I went off to the country, to a house that my parents-in-law had. And that's where I spent the war. All of it.

Men? There was a very nice man called Tim. He was married, though, and we were just friends – there was nothing more to it than that. I thought at one stage that he felt something more, and that it could have gone the other way, but it never did: I would not have allowed it. I remembered what the Frenchwoman had done to me and I could not do it to his wife, who was stuck over in Cardiff with an invalid aunt. And there was an American officer, also air force. He played the clarinet in the orchestra for almost eight months, and he came to see me at the house. He came from a place called Des Moines, which people said was in the middle of nowhere, but which he described as if it were Eden itself. He was charming; he amused me, and I liked him a great deal, but again I held back from any involvement.

Why? Well, I think that it had something to do with Feliks. I suppose if I'm honest with myself, I have to say that I had fallen in love with Feliks. He was reserved with me, and I thought at first that he didn't like me, but then I realised that this was just the way he was with everyone. He was very formal, very polite in an old-fashioned way.

I thought of him so much. When I woke up in the morning he was in my mind, and my first thought was whether I would see him that day. And if I did see him, if we talked or had any sort of contact, it was as if the day had been sanctified, rendered holy by his presence. Absurd? Of course it was, but love is an absurd phenomenon, utterly and completely different from any other state of mind. Do you know the feeling? You must do. It's as if the world has changed about you. Everything seems more vital, more charged. That's how it was. In the middle of that seemingly endless, ghastly battle with shortages and cold and, in my case, hungry foxes, everything is suddenly changed. Had he shown any sign of affection for me – in that way – then I'm sure that we would have been lovers. But he did not. And so I watched him from afar, as some women have to do; they wait upon the man they love, discreetly, and in fear of rejection, like somebody worshipping a god whom they can't quite see.

There was an issue. That's the best way I can describe it – and he had to go away. They took him off to do sensitive work near Cambridge and I did not see him again until, well, it was right at the end. VE Day, more or less – a few days afterwards, in fact. Do you remember the atmosphere then? How things were? My little orchestra had scraped its way through the entire war, and now it had come to an end we decided to hold a victory concert. That was when it happened. That was when I saw him again.

But do you know something? Do you know what I think of

myself? I think here I am at the age of forty-five, by myself. Men liked me. I was young enough during the war and immediately afterwards. It could have been different. But I think: here you are, one of those who have missed the bus.

Twenty-three

L a remembered how at the beginning, before the war really got going, they had spoken, half·in jest but half seriously, about a victory concert. Superstition had taken over, and there had been no such hubristic talk after that, until April 1945, when one of the sisters from Bury whispered to La – this sister for some reason always whispered when addressing La: 'La, it's getting close, I think. Maybe the orchestra should be ready.'

She agreed, but said that they would not talk about it just yet. 'I'll look out some pieces. I'll find something.'

They would avoid triumphalism, she thought; there would be opportunity enough for that elsewhere. Their victory concert would be one that would give people the chance to think about what they had been through. There would be something reflective, something peaceful, and perhaps, at one point, just silence for a few minutes. Music on either side of a silence made that silence all the more powerful, all the more moving.

The moment itself was really a series of moments. She happened to hear the news flash: the brief sound of bells and then the words, *The German Radio has just announced that Hitler is dead*. She sat down and folded her hands on her lap. She stood up and then sat down again. She did not know what to do. It seemed to her that everything would now stop; everything had been geared to this moment, for year after year, and now it had arrived. What would there be to do?

She barely slept, and was bone-tired when she went to deal with the hens. Henry produced a bottle of brandy and poured her half a glass. He had been drinking already, and his words were slurred. He kissed her on the cheek, and she smelled the alcohol on his breath.

'You won't leave the hens now, will you?' he asked.

'I haven't thought about it,' she said. 'I don't want to look after them forever.'

'I understand. But please . . . please not just yet.'

She sipped cautiously at her brandy; it was not a drink that she liked. They listened to the prime minister together. La closed her eyes as the familiar voice spoke to them; she heard the words, but her mind wandered; she felt only gratitude that he was there, that he had lived to see this moment. She conjured up a mental picture of a man in a tank suit and slippers, smiling at her. Comfortable, slightly eccentric, kind; it was Mr Churchill she saw, but it was also England.

We may allow ourselves a brief period of rejoicing, said Mr Churchill.

She called on the Aggs. Mrs Agg said, 'I can't believe it, Mrs Stone. I just can't.'

'Well it's true.'

Lennie came into the room. 'Good, isn't it?' he muttered. 'Old Hitler's dead now.'

La rose to her feet and embraced him, planting a kiss on his cheek. He smelled slightly sour; the smell of clothes that were not washed frequently enough. She spoke on impulse. 'Our orchestra is going to have a victory concert, Lennie. Would you like to play?'

He looked at her in astonishment. 'Me? I can't play.'

'But you like Billy Cotton, don't you? You must be musical. You could play the drums. We need somebody for that. Our percussionist would like some help. She'll tell you what to do.'

Mrs Agg watched anxiously. 'Go on, Lennie.'

He looked at his mother, and she nodded.

'All right. I'll play.'

La's orchestra performed its concert for victory a few days after VE Day. Word got out in the area and more people came than there were seats. The concert was on a Saturday afternoon, a warm day for that time of year. There were spring flowers on the banks and at the edge of the fields; the trees were coming into leaf. The Bury paper had mentioned the event – *Small orchestra plans big concert* – and there had been a brief piece in the *Cambridge Daily News*. It was this report that Feliks had seen, and that had brought him to the concert, arriving slightly later than the other players. He slipped in unnoticed by La, and he shared a music stand and music with another flautist, a driver from the base, who had recently joined the orchestra.

La looked up and saw Feliks just before they began the first piece – she had been busy handing out sheet music to one or two of the other players. For a few moments she stood quite still. Then Feliks looked up and their eyes met. He mouthed the word *Hello*. She nodded, and smiled. She did not show her feelings.

They started the concert. Tim stood up and made a short speech. He said, 'I am one of those who are grateful to La for keeping our little orchestra going through thick and thin. I knew one day that we would have this victory concert, but obviously I did not know when it would be. I thought it might be two years; then I thought three. It's been almost five. Now we are here to celebrate what has happened over the last few days and to think about some of the members of this orchestra who cannot be here because they have given their lives for their country – for their countries – and for peace.'

The hall was quiet as he read out three names. There was a young airman from Lancaster – still a boy, at eighteen, who had played the trombone, and who had been teased at the base because he admitted to never having had a girlfriend; there was a Canadian mechanic, a man from Nova Scotia, a quiet man who talked only of fishing; and a man from Des Moines, who had played the clarinet, and who had been shot down over Holland.

Tim sat down. La did not want to be thanked, but the audience was clapping her now, including those who were standing outside, listening through the door because there were not enough seats to be had. They all applauded. She looked out, over the heads of the players. She saw Feliks, who had laid his flute on his lap and was clapping too.

It was not easy for her to get through the programme. At the end, when the orchestra played 'Jerusalem' and people started to sing, La cried. She continued to conduct, though, and made it to the end, when she turned and faced the audience and bowed.

Afterwards, there was tea and cake served from tables at the side of the hall. The village had baked for days, and every sultana and cherry for miles around had been committed to the purpose. She found herself talking to Tim, and could tell from his eyes that he had cried too.

'Dab's here,' he said. 'Did you see him?'

She looked through the milling crowd. The whole village, together with everyone from the surrounding farms, was there. And there were at least thirty people from the air base, many in uniform. Where was Feliks?

She saw him near the door, talking to an airman. She slipped through the crowd until she was standing behind him.

'Feliks?'

He turned round slowly. She waited a moment, and then moved forward and put her arms round him.

'Thank you for coming,' she said. 'I wish I had known.'

'I read about it in the paper,' he said. 'I had to come.'

'Of course.'

She disengaged from the embrace and they stood facing one another.

'You don't blame me, do you?' she asked.

He hesitated, but she knew from his expression that he knew what she was talking about. 'I did. But not now.'

'I didn't know what to do,' she said. 'I was very confused.'

'It was a confusing time,' he said. 'But all that's over now.'

She saw him glance at his watch and she searched desperately for something to keep him. But she could not think of anything.

'Will you come and see me again?' she asked.

He pulled at the sleeves of his shirt. 'One day, maybe. I don't know where I'm going to be, though.'

'Of course you don't. But you know how to get in touch with me.'

Tim had come over and was shaking hands with Feliks. La moved away. The friend of the man from Des Moines was standing not far away and she wanted to speak to him, as she imagined that he would be going off somewhere else now and there were things that she needed to say to him, even if there was nothing more she could say to Feliks.

Part Three

Twenty-four

Tim left the base two months later, when he was given early demobilisation to take up a job with a civilian aircraft manufacturer in Bristol. Nothing had been said explicitly about disbanding the orchestra, but somehow everybody had assumed that this was what would happen. With Tim's departure, it was inevitable, and La wrote a short letter to everybody telling them that her orchestra had served its purpose. Tim came to see her the day before he left.

'We had a good innings,' he said. 'But I suppose it's time now, isn't it? What are you going to do, La?'

She had not thought about that. The euphoria and the air of unreality of the previous few weeks had kept her from planning a future for herself, and there was an element of denial too. Now, without thinking about it, she replied, 'Oh, I shall probably go and live in London for a while.'

'Lucky you. Theatre, and all that. Proper orchestras.'

'I imagine that it'll take a bit of time to get used to it again.'

She had not entertained the idea of moving back to London

– not since Valerie had put her off at the beginning of the war – but the idea must have been there, subconsciously, as it had popped up so readily. She could do it. Richard's parents had died during the war, within a year of one another, and their house in Chiswick, along with a substantial part of their estate, had come to her. She had already been comfortably-off financially, and the money made no real difference. But the house was empty, looked after by their housekeeper, and she could move in whenever she wished. She could keep the Suffolk house, of course, as a weekend place; people would start to do that sort of thing again, now that the war was over. She could get the garden under control again; she would not need to grow so many vegetables, and she would be released from the hens . . . That, in itself, was reason enough to go, she thought. And she could get a job – a real job this time – something that would allow her to use her mind.

The plan grew. She visited the house in Chiswick, passing through a London landscape that shocked her in its drabness and destruction. Entire streets had disappeared, others had wide gaps in them where buildings had disappeared. After Suffolk, where at least there was the high sky and the air, London seemed pinched and run-down, battered by what had happened to it.

She was shown round the house by the housekeeper. It had been kept clean, but there was in it that coldness that comes when the inhabiting spirit leaves a building. She saw Richard's room, which his mother had kept as a shrine to him, as parents will do. It was the room of a teenage boy; a cricket bat on the wall, school photographs, even a teddy-bear propped up on the shelf above the small fireplace. The housekeeper stood back, in sympathy, when she looked into this room, and when La came out of it she said, 'I could clear that out for you, you know. It must be painful.'

La nodded. 'Thank you.'

'And I could be out of my rooms in a week or two. I could go up north . . .'

'You don't have to leave, Mrs Eaton. You can stay. There's so much room here. You can stay.'

She made arrangements, and two months later La moved from Suffolk to Chiswick. For a couple of weeks she organised the house, making it fresher and more habitable. Mrs Eaton kept the kitchen, and proved to be a competent cook. She made evening meals for La, which she left in a warming oven with a note as to the menu. It was like living in a hotel, thought La, but she had a roof over her head – a large one – and there were so many in London who were living in cramped and unsanitary conditions. And she was alive. As Tim had said, that was the important thing.

She found a job. A small music publisher wanted a person to assist its manager. They specialised in the publication of collections of traditional songs, and they needed somebody who could turn a hand to any of the tasks associated with that. At her interview, La was shown their latest project, a collection of folk songs from the British Isles. The page proofs fell open at 'Brigg Fair'.

'We played that,' she remarked. 'I had a little orchestra in Suffolk. Very amateurish. We played that during the war.' She turned the page. 'And here's "Scarborough Fair"'.

She glanced at the familiar words. *Remember me to one who lives there/She once was a true love of mine.*

The manager was looking at her across his desk. 'Cambridge,' he said.

'You too?'

'Yes. Do you remember Paulson's Music Shop? We deal with him. He's a stockist of ours.'

She said that she did. And she remembered the buying of the flute, and the way that Feliks held it when she first gave it to him. *I would have given you anything*, she said to herself. *Anything*.

The manager closed the file in front of him. 'It seems to me that you would be just the person for this job, Mrs Stone,' he said. 'Now, as to salary. I'm afraid that with conditions as they are . . .'

'That is not really a factor,' said La. 'Please don't worry about that.'

The job was perfect. When friends asked her, she described it as a 'small job', which it was, but it suited her ideally. The office, which was just off Russell Square, near the British Museum, was small and chaotic, filled with scores and proofs of scores and letters to arrangers and composers. La succeeded in bringing some order to it, and was promoted. She was given a new room, with a carpet, and a two-bar fire. From her window she looked out onto a small square of garden and a low wall on which pigeons settled and conducted their courtships. At weekends, she went to the house in Suffolk; Mrs Agg would air it for her just before she arrived and make a fire in the range. Lennie cut the hedges and mowed the grass in summer. He talked to her now, and told her that he had somebody he called his 'sweetheart', a young woman from a neighbouring village. He would marry her one day, he said; maybe when he was forty or thereabouts.

'You should marry again, Mrs Stone,' said Mrs Agg. 'I hope you don't mind my saying that. But you're an attractive woman and there must be men enough in London.'

La laughed. 'I'm forty-one now, Mrs Agg. Who wants a woman of forty-one?'

'A man of forty-two, I'd say. Are there any of them in London?'

From time to time, she heard from Tim, and even saw him on occasion, when he came to London on business, and they would go for lunch in a Soho restaurant. They talked about the war, and the orchestra, and he told her the news from the aviation world, which meant little to her. Then, on one of these occasions, he suddenly said to her, 'You know, La, there's something I feel really bad about. Looking back . . . all right, we were all doing a job and we did it to the best of our ability. Nothing to be ashamed of in that. But I feel bad about the Poles.'

She looked surprised. 'But I always thought that you went out of your way to help them. Look what you did for Feliks.' He had been kind to him; she had seen that herself.

'Oh, it's not me personally. No, it's what we as a people did. We betrayed them.'

'Yalta?'

'Yes. Of course, there was that. I remember after the news got out, the Poles at the station just sat. They looked as if they'd been winded. And quite a few of us felt that we just couldn't look them in the eye. We had to look the other way, because we knew what they were going through. We had just given their country to the very enemy who had joined in with the Germans in dismembering it. We gave it to the people who had been allies of Nazi Germany.'

La agreed. But she pointed out it had not been easy to deal with Stalin. Roosevelt had wanted them to join in the war against Japan; he had to give them something. She sighed; the world was rotten. 'Yalta was a disaster. Yes, I know. But what else could they do? How could they . . .' She searched for words, but none came. At the heart of the machinations of statesmen were greed and fear and a seeking of advantage. But could one say that without sounding completely cynical?

Tim was watching her. 'Yalta,' he said, 'was the big sell-out. But there were other things too. Do you remember the Victory parade in London? Did you see it?'

La had. She had watched it alone, in the rain, and afterwards had walked into an unfamiliar tea-room and sat for an hour before she had gone home. She had thought about how it must seem to those who had lost somebody and who were watching the parade. How did they feel when they saw everybody else parading but their husband, their father, their son or daughter. She replied simply. 'I did.'

Tim looked at her enquiringly. 'And who wasn't there?'

La knew. 'The Poles.'

'Exactly. We didn't let them – let those brave men – march alongside everybody else because Stalin had said they were not to be in the parade. Our parade – not his. Ours. And do you know something, La? I had a letter from one of them who said to me that he watched the parade in tears. He had to stand on the pavement because there was no place for him or any of his fellow Poles in that parade.'

He watched the effect of his words. La looked down at the tablecloth.

'And do you know something else?' Tim continued. 'Some of our politicians called the Poles fascists. They were so much in love with their hero Stalin and his beloved Soviet Union that they took their cue from the very Russians who had murdered all those Polish officers – lined them up and shot them. Or had carted people off to die in their labour camps.' He shook his head. 'No wonder, La. No wonder the Poles felt betrayed. They fought for a country that they would never be able to return to. They lost everything. No pensions. Nothing. All gone.'

'But what makes me sick at heart, La, is the thought of those men watching the parade. They had fought in the Battle of Britain, with us, right beside us, and they were forbidden to take part in the parade. Because of some Russian butcher. That's what sickens me – that more than anything else. The thought of those men standing there in tears. Attlee . . . well, but how could Churchill have allowed that?'

La thought: doesn't he remember? 'He had no power.'

'Or the King?'

La shrugged. 'Even less power.'

Tim looked away, and La reached out to lay her hand on his forearm. 'I'm sure that Feliks would have understood.'

'Would he?' Tim asked. 'Do you really think so?'

'Possibly not.'

They talked about Feliks. 'I've often thought,' Tim said, 'that you and Feliks might have been . . . suited. You were very friendly, weren't you?' He smiled encouragingly. 'Was there ever anything between you?'

La held his gaze. 'Nothing. Not really.'

'Pity.'

In the late summer of 1960, La went to Edinburgh, to the Festival. She travelled up with her friend Valerie, who was at a loose end because her husband was in Australia on business. They decided that they would spend ten days there, at concerts and at the theatre. They had different tastes and so they did not go to the same events, but they had each other's company for dinner.

On the evening before they were due to return to London. La went by herself to an orchestral concert at the Usher Hall. At the end of the concert, there was still some light in the northern sky, and the evening was a warm one. The audience spilled out onto the pavement in front of the hall, talking about the programme, exchanging the welled-up small talk that concert audiences release at the end of a performance. La stood for a moment on the steps, enjoying the festival feel of the occasion, and it was then that she saw Feliks.

He had come out of a side door and was about to walk up Lothian Road when he stopped and turned to face her. It seemed that he was hesitant to approach her, but she made the first move and took a few steps towards him.

They shook hands. It was very formal.

She smiled at him, hoping that he could not hear her wildly beating heart. 'I thought it was you.'

'And it is. Fifteen years later? Yes, fifteen.'

He seemed pleased to see her, in spite of the formality.

'Where . . .' she began to ask. But he cut her short.

'I live in Glasgow now. I've lived there since the end of the war. I was offered a job there by a Pole who had set up a business.'

'Oh.'

She did not look for it, but she saw the ring. He noticed.

'Yes. I married a Scottish lady. Twelve years ago. We have two small boys. One is five and the other is seven.'

La tried to smile. Again he noticed. He could see the effort.

'My marriage is not a success,' he said. 'She calls herself a Catholic, but she is a rather bad Catholic, I'm afraid. I see her every few weeks – she comes to visit the boys – but she is living with a man who has a bar.' He shrugged. 'That is how it is.'

'I'm very sorry to hear that.'

He nodded. 'Not good. But you – where are you?'

'I am in London.'

'And you are happy there?'

'Yes. But I still go out to Suffolk. I still have the house.'

His eyes lit up. 'With the lavender bushes?'

'Yes. They need cutting back, I think.'

They both laughed. Then La said, 'Feliks, I have to ask you. If I don't ask you now, then I may never know. Do you know why I had to speak to Tim as I did? Do you understand?'

Behind them a woman said something to a man in a dinner jacket and the man chuckled. Feliks glanced at the couple and then back at La. 'Yes, I do understand. You knew that I was German.'

It took her a moment to grasp what he said.

'So I was right?'

'Yes. But you were kind to me and you did nothing about it. You see . . .' He looked over his shoulder, as if concerned that he might be overheard. 'You see, my parents were Germans who went to live in Poland. My father was a businessman. I was eight when they went and I went to school there. I learned Polish and spoke it all the time. We stayed, and then when I went to university I decided that I would be Polish altogether. What is the first eight years of your life? Not very much. The Nazis had come to power then in Germany. I had no desire to go back. Then I joined the air force. I took the identity of a man who had worked for my father and who had died. I joined the air force under his name.'

She reached out and took his hand. He did not resist; they held hands.

'It seemed clear to me,' he continued. 'If I tried to explain to people who I really was, they would have been suspicious. When I ended up in England, they would probably have interned me.'

He was right. People were interned indiscriminately. 'Yes, that could have happened.'

'It was simpler to be Polish,' he said. 'Which is what I felt, and what I feel now.'

She wanted to hug him.

'I understand,' she said. 'I understand.'

'They found all this out in London, but the man who interrogated me was sympathetic. He had a German grandfather and he knew that we were not all monsters. He gave me clearance and they found work for me.'

'So,' she said.

'Yes. So.'

He looked at his watch. 'I have to get back to Glasgow. The boys are being looked after tonight by the wife of a friend. But I have to get the last train back.' He reached for a pen from his jacket pocket and started to write on the back of his programme. 'Here is my address in Glasgow. Perhaps one day we shall be able to meet again.'

She took the programme for him, and put it in her bag. She felt tears in her eyes and turned away. It is always like this, she thought; I cry. He pressed her hand briefly, and was gone.

Twenty-five

The following year, in 1961, the year of La's fiftieth birthday, the music publishers were acquired by a larger firm, competitors who had eyed them for some years and were now in a position to make an offer that the handful of shareholders in the smaller company found sufficiently attractive. Nobody's job was threatened, the new owners said, but people would have to be prepared to be flexible. La was told that she was still needed, but that she would have to move to a smaller office in a new building. The old premises, with their view of the small garden and the wall, with their creaky staircase and their staff coffee-room with the Georgian cornice, were too valuable to keep and would be sold.

La resigned. She would miss the job, but she did not need to work; and London was becoming more of an effort, with its crowds and its noise. A hotel had opened near her house in Chiswick, and its bar was a source of disturbance at night. She decided to go back to Suffolk, keeping the London house for when she wanted to spend time in town. Mrs Eaton had long since retired; she could find a lodger who would look after it, a student nurse perhaps, somebody like that.

Agg had retired, and sat in the kitchen all day, complaining to Mrs Agg about the weather and the government, and other matters too. Lennie ran the farm, and had married the woman he called his sweetheart. She got on well with her mother-in-law, and they seemed happy enough. 'You can't make a farmer's wife,' said Mrs Agg. 'You're born to it or you're not. Lennie's sweetheart was born to it.'

Henry Madder was in a wheelchair, but had stayed where he was; no Madder had ever gone anywhere, he claimed. A nephew on his wife's side had taken over the running of his farm and had got rid of the hens, using the wood from the hen houses to patch up fences and gates. The pig farmer had died in a fall from his horse. Percy Brown had become a sergeant and had left the force to drive a taxi in Bury in his retirement. He picked up La from the station one day and told her that his one outstanding ambition had never been fulfilled: to catch one of the gypsies from Foster's Field red-handed. 'They were too wily for me,' he said. 'Our problem in the police was always proof. Still is, I suppose.'

La hoped that Feliks would get in touch with her, but he did not. She sent him a Christmas card that December, and told him that she had moved back to Suffolk. With the card she sent him a newspaper cutting about an amateur orchestra in Norwich. 'I thought you might find this interesting,' she wrote at the top of the report. 'Remember how it was.'

La thought about peace. She had been born just before the first war, and had been seven when it ended. She remembered the

Armistice as a time of bells and strange, adult rejoicing. She remembered tears and solemnity. Then there had been her own war, the one which she knew had involved such a narrow escape. She had seen the estimates of the number killed: the mind could hardly contemplate those tens of millions, all those wasted, curtailed lives; all that misery. And then, after all that, an arms race that threatened to obscure the losses of the first fifty years of the century; this could destroy all human life, pulverise continents, darken the skies for centuries. And that apocalyptic vision was not fantasy; it was real. They could work out – and had done so – how many tons of dynamite there were for each of our human lives, for every one of us. She awoke sometimes at night and thought of this. But it cannot happen, she told herself. Humanity could not be so stupid.

But it almost did happen. The world had become divided into two hostile camps, each bristling with arms, each warily guarding its appointed patch, marking out territory with barbed wire and towers. In one of these camps, people lived under the thumb of a tsar in modern clothing, serfs to an ideology that sought to bend human nature to its particular vision; in the other, human nature could be itself, but that brought injustice and exploitation, not always held in check by the values proclaimed by the rhetoric of freedom. La saw the world change before her eyes; people relaxed, dressed less formally, spoke about the end of the old oppressive structures that had held people down in ways subtle and unsubtle. But for her, life seemed unchanged, barely touched by the movements and shifts of the times. Again I have missed it, she thought; heady things are happening, and I am not there; I am somewhere in the wings, watching what is happening on the stage, in a play in which I have no real part.

That is what my life has been. Even in my marriage, Richard's heart was elsewhere. I have been a handmaiden; she relished the word – a handmaiden; one who waits and watches; assists, perhaps, but only in a small way.

Standing in her kitchen in the house in Suffolk, one afternoon in late summer, she looked out of her window, over the fields on the other side of the road and to the sky beyond. Clouds had built up, heavy purple banks; rain would reach her soon – it was already falling on the ploughed fields to the east, a veil of it drifting down, caught in the slanting afternoon light, white against the inky bulk of the clouds behind. She stood quite still, transfixed by the moment; as happens sometimes, when we are not expecting it; we stop and think about the beauty of the world, and its majesty, and the insignificance of our concerns and cares. And yet we know that they are not insignificant – at least not to us; pain and loss may be little things *sub specie aeternitatis* but to us, even in our ultimate insignificance, they loom large, are wounding, are sore. So each of us, thought La, each one of us should do something to make life better for somebody, to change the course of events, even if only in the most local sense. Even a handmaiden can do something about that.

The moment passed. La had become accustomed to an uneventful life; a life of reading, of listening to music, of occasional entertaining of friends from London. She travelled to Italy, taking guided art tours in groups of like-minded people. Friendships developed on these trips, but even when addresses were exchanged at the end, and promises were made to keep in touch, this rarely happened. La did not mind; she was lonely, but had accepted loneliness as her lot. There were her authors and her composers; they kept her company; Bach, Mozart, Rossini were always at hand, did not let her down.

A friend passed her literature on the Campaign for Nuclear Disarmament. She read the leaflets and thought: everything they say here is true. We cannot use these weapons; nobody can. But she knew that there were those who did not think this way, and that some of these people, many of them, in fact, were generals and military strategists. For them, atomic weapons were simply another item in their bulging armamentarium – a powerful item, but one that had a trigger that could be pulled in the same way as any other trigger.

She joined a march from Aldermaston, where these weapons were developed, to London, to stand in Trafalgar Square in a crowd of almost one hundred thousand people and listen to the call for the rejection of these ways of killing us all. She was not a pacifist, and argued quite strongly with a man who walked beside her on the march. He said that humanity would never restrain itself in war, and that the only solution was to eschew war altogether; he said that, with all the conviction of his eighteen or nineteen years. But he was too young, she felt, to remember what it was like to be faced with evil that is intent on fulfilling itself.

'What about Hitler?' she said.

'People always ask that question,' he said. 'Like the rabbit out of the hat. What about Hitler?'

'Well,' said La. 'What about him? What would you have done?'

'Reasoned with him. Shown him and everybody like him that violence gets you nowhere.'

She stared at him. Someone on the other side of the column

of marchers was singing, and the words of the song were being taken up by others.

'That would not have worked,' she said. 'It would not have stopped Belsen. It would not have stopped Auschwitz. The only way to stop those was to fight those who created them.'

'And kill them?'

'Yes,' said La. 'I suppose so.'

He looked at her scornfully. 'Then what are you doing here?' he asked, and moved away to walk with somebody else. La thought: perhaps he does not really know; perhaps Auschwitz is just a name to him, like the name of any other place in the history of other people.

That autumn, the Russians exploded a fifty-megaton bomb above an Arctic island. This was four thousand times as powerful as the bomb dropped on Hiroshima. La read about it in the newspapers and sat in silence. She remembered as a child a boy who lived a few houses away who loved fireworks. She had watched him once when he had tied ten squibs together to make a more powerful explosion. She had seen the light in his eyes, the enthusiasm, and had been aware, for the first time in her life, that there was something very different about the way in which boys thought. This came back to her now.

And then, the following year, it all almost came true. It happened so quickly; the photographic evidence was pinned up and pointed to by indignant politicians. The Russians were placing missiles in Cuba that would enable them to strike the United States at short range. Demands were made, and positions taken. Two deadly enemies, each capable of destroying the other, and everyone else with them, faced one another over a chess board of bristling missiles. When the news sank in, and what it could mean, La went

out into her garden and stood for a moment, silent under the sky.
The leaves had fallen and the garden was braced for winter; somewhere, high above her head, there was an aeroplane; the droning
of its engine seemed ominous now, just as that same sound had
been ominous exactly twenty years previously.

La thought: there is nothing that anybody can do. We are
powerless. Last time, when evil incarnate threatened us, we could
do something – and did. We each did something, even if it was
only looking after hens. The world was smaller, more personal
then; now there is nothing that any of us can do. This is being
decided by machines with blinking lights; by radar screens; by
the switches and levers of a world that has ceased to have anything
to do with an ordinary person standing in her garden.

On the day after President Kennedy addressed the American
people and the full gravity of the Cuban situation came to be
understood, La sat down and drew up a list of those members
of her orchestra with whom she was still in touch, or whose telephone number she knew. It came to twelve names, including
Tim, Feliks, and the two sisters from Bury. She telephoned them
all that afternoon and evening.

'Do you remember our victory concert?' she said.

Of course they did.

'I want to hold a concert for peace,' she said. 'In five days'
time. I know that it's not much notice, but there isn't much time,
I'm afraid.'

She asked people to contact other members of the orchestra
and pass on the message. Everyone she spoke to said they would
participate; nobody said that he or she could not come. Leave
was taken. It was too important to say no, and they felt that they
owed this to La.

She prepared the hall, helped by Mrs Agg. Lennie put up notices, and the sisters in Bury spoke to the vicar of their parish, who passed the word around his congregation, and around others.

On the morning of the concert, La awoke early and walked in her garden, nursing a cup of tea. She looked up at the sky. If the end were to come, it would be the end of everything – the end of music, the end of her house, of Suffolk, of the birds, of lavender bushes, of England. She stood quite still and put her empty tea-cup down on the stone bench beside the pond she had created the previous year. A small frog launched itself into the water; it would be the end of frogs, and of whales, and of the sea itself.

They gathered in the tin hall. Many people came – so many that, as at the victory concert, there were people standing outside. The atmosphere was grave. They were silent; nobody talked or smiled as they had done in 1945.

La stood at the podium. She had chosen the music carefully, and although they had not had time to rehearse, and although so many were rusty, they played to the best of their ability, and the audience listened with solemnity. Nobody clapped in between the pieces. They were silent.

It could have been a time for gravity, for music in the minor keys of sadness and farewell, for that, in large part, is how people felt when the concert began. It hit them abruptly, and with shocking force: this could so easily be good-bye. They had lived with that knowledge ever since mushroom clouds first started to rise in the sky; they knew that a rash decision, a moment of reckless anger in the mind of a powerful man could bring the world to an end. It was almost impossible to absorb that knowledge, yet people had done so. But that was not really why La had called the concert. She had called it because she believed in the power of music. Absurdly, irrationally, she believed that music could make a difference to the temper of the world. She did not investigate this belief, test it to see whether it made sense; she simply believed it, and so she chose music that expressed order and healing; Bach for order; Mozart for healing. This was the antithesis of the anger and fear that could unleash the missiles; this was music showing the face of love, and forgiveness.

And then, near the end, somebody outside shouted, and the shout came through the door and into the hall. Somebody had heard, and was spreading the news. Mr Krushchev had made a speech on Moscow Radio. They were not going to die.

They stopped. People dropped their instruments. They embraced one another. They cried. Lennie hit his drums enthusiastically in one long, powerful roll that threatened to burst the instruments' skins. Nobody worried. The loss of drums was nothing to the loss of the world. They laughed.

La walked back to her house. She would return to the hall, where a party had broken out, but she wanted to go back and fetch a coat, for it had turned cold. She was in her kitchen, preparing to return to the hall, when the car came into the drive. It was Feliks.

He got out of the car, and his two small boys were with him. She had seen him in the hall, and they had exchanged a few words, but she had not seen the boys. They looked so like Feliks, she thought; his two sons with those serious expressions that only small boys can have.

'I wanted to see you,' he said.

'And you've brought your boys.'

'Yes, these are my boys.'

They sat in the kitchen, where they had sat together so many times all those years ago. The boys played outside, some odd little game that involved the one chasing the other. 'They can play like that for hours,' he said. 'Boys. So much energy.'

'I don't suppose they have any idea of the danger we've been through,' said La. 'Fortunately for them.'

Feliks nodded. 'Sometimes we don't have an idea of the danger we're in. Did we? During the War? Did we really know how close it came?'

'Perhaps we did. But we couldn't really lead our lives thinking about it. We had to believe that we were going to be all right.' She paused. 'You said something a long time ago. You said something about having to believe or we wouldn't be able to continue. Do you remember that conversation?'

'No. I remember that we talked about a lot of things. But I don't remember that.'

'Well you did. And I think that I said something about how we could find courage in unexpected places. Something like that.'

They were silent.

'And now, here we are again.' He looked at her. 'Happy or unhappy, as the case may be. Content with the way our lives have worked out. Which is it, La? Which is it for you?'

'Happy,' she said. 'Or happy enough. Some parts of my life have been unhappy.'

He seemed to be waiting for her to say something more. He raised an eyebrow. 'And can you tell me? Do you want to?'

Of course, she thought. Of course I do.

'I might have been happier if I had had children.'

He looked away. 'Yes, I understand.'

'And if I had been a better musician.' She laughed, and he did too.

'You still have time to improve,' he said. 'You could start your orchestra again.'

She did not think that she could. 'There was a special time for that,' she said. 'Not now.'

'Maybe not.'

The silence returned. The kitchen door had been pushed open by a small hand, and the boys had returned. The smaller one had fallen and there was mud on the knees of his trousers. La got up and fetched a damp cloth from the sink. 'I'll do that for you,' she said to the boy. 'Come over here. I'll fix you up.'

Felix watched. When she had finished wiping off the mud, the boy took a step backwards. He was shy.

Felix spoke. 'La, your orchestra has saved the world – again.'

She made a self-deprecatory gesture. 'I don't know about that,' she said.

'I do,' he said.

She reached out to ruffle the hair of the smaller boy, who had been staring at her with wide eyes. 'What are you going to do now?' she asked Feliks. 'Go back to Glasgow?'

'Yes. I suppose I should.'

She drew breath. In the face of the end of everything, even if the threat had suddenly passed, one might say what one had always wanted to say. That is what she thought.

'Stay with me,' she said. 'You could stay here. I think we would be happy.'

Feliks held her gaze, and she looked into his eyes. Then he glanced at the boys. 'But . . .'

'All of you,' she said.

And she picked up the boys, one after the other, and kissed them.

ALEXANDER MCCALL SMITH is the author of the international phenomenon The No. 1 Ladies' Detective Agency series, the Isabel Dalhousie series, the Portuguese Irregular Verbs series, and the 44 Scotland Street series. He is professor emeritus of medical law at the University of Edinburgh in Scotland and has served on many national and international bodies concerned with bioethics. He lives in Scotland.